UPON MY SOUL

UPON MY SOUL

BY
ROBERT J. RANDISI

December 2013

Down and Out Books, LLC
3959 Van Dyke Rd, Ste. 265
Lutz, FL 33558
www.DownAndOutBooks.com

Cover art and design by JT. Linroos

ISBN: 1-937495-65-5

ISBN-13: 978-1-937495-65-7

To Marthayn,

the only one who knows *my* soul

Upon my soul,
upon my free and joyous soul,
guard me when old Satan's nigh,
upon my soul.

—Townes Van Zandt

PRELUDE

The day Sangster woke and discovered he had a soul after all, everything changed.

But along with the soul came a conscience, something else he had never experienced in his thirty-seven years. He was not awake five minutes when he began to weep. He wept not only for the people he'd killed over the years, but for their families, who had been deprived of their loved ones. He wept uncontrollably, and it was a day of firsts, for he had never cried before, not even as a child.

Sangster was a new man, but the question became...was he a better man?

He left his apartment that day and never returned. In fact, no one in California ever saw him again, and for many years he was presumed dead. Those who knew him figured that his line of work had finally caught up with him.

It seemed logical to assume that a man who was an assassin for hire would fall prey to an assassin, himself.

But that was not the case...

ONE
Three Years Later...

Sangster looked up from the chessboard at the man who had appeared at the end of his front walk. In the almost three years he had been renting this house on Algiers Point—one of the neighborhoods left dry by Hurricane Katrina located across Lake Ponchatrain from the French Quarter—the only person who had ever come up that walk was his neighbor, with whom he played chess at least three times a week.

"Know 'im?" Ken Burke asked.

Sangster glanced across the table at the older man, who had not looked up from the board.

"Yeah," he said, "I know him."

The man advanced up the walk carefully, as if he expected somebody to take a shot at him at any moment. He probably would have felt better if he knew Sangster hadn't touched a gun in three years.

When he reached the porch he stopped and stared at Sangster before he spoke.

"Hello, Sangster."

"Primble."

Burke looked up at that, eyed Sangster, who could only shrug his shoulders.

"What do you want?"

"A lot of people think you're dead," Primble said.

"That was kind of the idea, Eddie."

"It worked pretty well," Eddie Primble said, "until now."

"Well, you didn't find me," Sangster said. "I know that much. Who was it?"

"Top secret," Primble said. "Is there someplace we can talk?"

"You don't want to talk in front of my friend?"

Primble looked at Ken Burke, who continued to eye the board intently.

"You have a friend?" he asked. "Things *have* changed quite a bit in three years."

Sangster looked at Primble.

"Yes, "he said, "they have." He looked at Burke. Primble had aged badly in three years. Sangster knew Primble must have been forty, but much of his hair had receded and he'd put on weight. He looked fifty— healthy enough, but fifty. The cut of his suit also bespoke of some progress financially. He was sweating. It was February, but that didn't mean much in New Orleans. It was still nearly ninety degrees.

"I have to talk to this man," he said to his chess opponent.

"Go ahead and talk," Burke said. "I'm concentratin'."

Sangster looked at Primble.

"He won't listen, he's concentrating."

"I intend to talk very plainly," Primble warned.

"Talk as plainly as you want," Sangster said. "I have no secrets from Burke."

"Your friend," Primble reiterated.

"And neighbor," Sangster said. "He lives in the house next door."

"How much does the old timer know?"

"Everything."

"Everything?" Burke asked. He ignored the "old timer" remark. After all, he was seventy. If that didn't qualify as an old timer, what did? "If I knew *everything*, this game would've been over a long time ago." Sangster knew—Primble did not—that Burke was not only talking about chess.

"Eddie," Sangster said, "you found me—or somebody found me for you. What do you want?"

"I need you," Primble said, "to...to do what you used to do."

"He wants you to kill somebody," Burke said, eyeing the board, chin in hand.

"That's what I used to do," Sangster said. He looked at Primble. "I don't do that anymore."

"You don't—come on, Sangster," Primble said. "What else does a man like you do?"

"I'm retired."

"Retired?"

"I don't kill anymore," he said. "I haven't killed anyone in three years. I don't even own a gun, and I haven't held one in all that time."

"You expect me to believe that?" Primble asked.

"I don't care what you believe, Eddie," Sangster told him. "It's the truth."

Primble thought a moment, put one foot up on the first step. It was warm, and he was sweating. He loosened his tie, undid the top button of his shirt.

"All right," he said. "For the moment let's assume that you haven't killed anyone in three years." He adopted a look of complete puzzlement. "Why not?"

"That's not important," the ex-assassin said. "All you need to know is that I don't do it anymore. You need to find someone else."

"Do you know how long it took me to find you?" Primble demanded.

"Let me guess," Sangster said. "Three years?"

"I'm not just gonna take no for an answer, Sangster," Primble said. "That's not what I do, remember?"

"I remember very well."

"In fact," the man went on, "when you walked out you left behind an unfinished assignment. I had to have someone else do your job for you."

"Luckily," Sangster replied, "you hadn't paid me in advance."

"That's not the point."

"I know," Sangster said. "I've been trying to get you to see the point, Eddie."

"Sangster," Primble said, "you were the best I ever ran."

"I'm out of the business, Eddie."

"You can't get out of this business, Sangster," Primble said. "Why don't we just call the last three years a vacation?"

Sangster looked at the chess board. The old man hadn't made a move yet. He had his chin in his left hand, and his right hand was down out of sight.

"Eddie—"

"You don't think I came alone, do you?" Primble asked.

"I don't really care if you came alone or not, Eddie," Sangster said. "You're leaving, either way."

"There are two guns trained on you right now. If I nod, you're dead, and your chess buddy, too."

It got quiet, and suddenly they all heard the sound of the hammer being cocked on a gun.

"I thought you said you didn't own a gun," Primble said.

"He don't," Ken Burke said. "I do."

Burke brought his right hand into sight. He was holding a big .45 Peacemaker, the kind they used to carry in the old west.

"You so much as twitch, let alone nod, and it'll be the last thing you ever do," Burke told Primble.

"Easy, old timer," Primble said. "That thing's pretty old. It might explode in your hand."

"I guess you don't really know much about guns, do ya, Mister?" Burke asked. "That probably comes from havin' other people do your killin' for ya. This here's a collector's item, and I keep it in pristine shape. It's the pride of my collection, and believe me when I tell you it's in fine workin' order."

That was the most Sangster thought he'd heard the older man say at one time in the almost three years he'd known him.

Primble was sweating even more, but it wasn't from the heat.

"Is he serious?" he asked.

"Dead serious," Sangster said. "Show him, Burke."

With his left hand Burke took his wallet from his pocket and flipped it open to show Primble his badge.

"You're a cop?"

"Sheriff," Burke said. "Retired, but I keep my hand in."

"Sangster," Primble said, "I just wanted to talk."

"Then you should have left the threats at home," Sangster said. "Come on." He stood up, as did Burke.

"Where we going?" Primble asked.

"You signal your boys to put up their guns," Sangster said. "We're going to walk you to the ferry, so nobody decides to take a shot at me."

"Look, I—"

"We're done talking, Eddie."

"I need you, Sangster!"

"You heard the man," Burke said. "Now give whatever signal you arranged so your men know to put up their guns."

Primble frowned, and for a moment looked like a man about to cry. Finally, he turned his body partially and waved his hand in disgust.

"They're leaving," he said.

"Good," Sangster said, "they'll be on the same ferry you're on. Let's go."

"I don't know why—" Burke prodded Primble in the back with the barrel of the Peacemaker and the man almost jumped out of his skin. They made the walk to the Algiers ferry in silence.

Sangster watched the ferry start across the lake back to New Orleans.

"You sure his men were on there, too?" Burke asked.

"I'm sure," Sangster said.

Sangster looked at the Peacemaker is his friend's hand.

"I'm glad you brought that over here today to show me."

"Yeah," Burke said, with a grin. He took it off cock and lowered it to his side.

"Would it really have fired?"

"To tell you the truth," Burke said, "I don't know." He waited a beat, then added, "Maybe if it'd been loaded.

TWO

On the ferry, Silk Guiliano and Jimmy O'Malley walked over to where Eddie Primble was sitting.

"What the hell happened?" Silk asked.

"Yeah," Jimmy said. "He run us off?"

"He did," Primble said. "He's still as good as ever. Wants me to believe he hasn't pulled the trigger—hell, even held a gun—in three years, but..." Primble shook his head in admiration. "He had that old man hold the gun. It was...brilliant."

Silk looked at Jimmy.

"He ran us off, and Eddie's impressed."

"I *ain't* so impressed," Jimmy replied. He looked at Primble. "Is the bet still on?"

"It's still on," Primble said. "I fingered him for you, didn't I? You both get a good look at him?"

"I did," Silk said. He was in his early thirties, dressed completely in black. He had christened himself "Silk" years ago, liking the name and all its connotations. "Smooth as silk," that's what he told women, and he also considered himself to be smooth as silk with a gun.

O'Malley, on the other hand, was just the opposite. Late twenties, he was rough, crude, but effective when it came to killing.

One of these men wanted to take the place of Sangster in Eddie Primble's operation, but Primble wouldn't pick one until he knew that Sangster was dead and not coming back. So a wager had been put in place, between Silk and Jimmy. Whichever man managed to kill Sangster would get his spot. The other man would be relegated to second banana, and neither man wanted that.

"So," Primble said, "you both know him on sight, the rest is up to you."

Silk and Jimmy exchanged a look, then Silk asked, "Are you sure you didn't talk him into coming back?"

"Yeah," Jimmy said. "Maybe you told him about us?"

"He says he's done with it," Primble said. "If he's truly finished, I can't have him running around out here alive, not with what he knows. No, he didn't agree to come back. He's your target, boys, and there's a lot at stake."

"He didn't look so tough," O'Malley said.

"Don't underestimate him," Primble said. "That's the only advice I'm going to give you both."

"I'm not going to underestimate him," Silk said. "What's the point of killing him if he's not the best?"

"Oh, he was the best all right," Primble said. "The best I ever saw. Probably still is."

"We'll see about that," Silk said, looking back at Algiers.

For want of something else to say, Jimmy O'Malley said, "Yeah."

THREE

It had taken Sangster a year to get to know Ken Burke well enough to tell him the truth. As a retired lawman, Burke didn't approve of the way Sangster had made his living, but as a man who had done his own share of killing—all in the line of duty, of course—he understood a man finding redemption. As a Christian, he forgave Sangster, and their friendship grew stronger after that.

They didn't finish their chess game after walking Primble to the ferry. Sangster told the old man he had some thinking to do.

"About leavin'?"

"Maybe."

"That'd be a shame."

"I know," Sangster said. He loved the house in Algiers. He also loved the French Quarter and everything it had to offer, from its great bookstores to its countless musical venues, its food and its women. Especially its women.

"Then don't let that feller ruin it."

"There's only one way I could be sure he won't, Burke."

"By killin' him?"

Sangster nodded.

"And I'm not going to do that."

"Got to be another way, then."

"That's what I'm going to think about."

"Well, gimme a shout if you need me," Burke said. "I got guns that I know *will* shoot."

"I'll keep that in mind. Thanks, Ken."

After his neighbor left, Sangster walked to one of the front windows and stared out. He had known someone would find him sooner or later, but he'd hoped it wouldn't be his old boss, Primble. Now he was either going to have to deal with the man, take care of him or move on and make a new life somewhere else. The only problem with the third one was he knew Primble wouldn't stop looking. He had too much invested in Sangster just to let him go, and if he could find him—or have him found—once, he could do it again.

The problem with the second option was that he didn't kill anymore.

So the only option left to him was number one, deal with him.

From his vantage point, he could see his mailbox, one of those big metal ones mounted on a pole and fitted with a red flag. When the flag was up, something was in the box. The flag had not been up in the three years he'd been living there, because nobody knew where he was to send him mail. He didn't even get junk mail because he'd instructed the post office never to deliver it.

Then why was the flag up now?

He went out the front door and down the walk to the mailbox. He saw that the door was slightly ajar. He hadn't thought about things like booby traps and trip wires for over two years.

That first year he'd kept expecting to find death around every corner, but eventually he was able to relax and start living a normal life—not "again," because he couldn't remember when he'd actually lived a normal life. Certainly not growing up. How normal could it have been to constantly be trying to avoid parents in his own house? And certainly not since he killed his first man at fifteen. So surely it had only been the past two years that he could call his life normal, by conventional standards.

Now, as he stared at the mailbox, he had to summon back some of those old instincts. He examined the pole and the box on the outside, then used his fingers to search for wires of any kind. Finally, after pressing his ear to the box and listening intently, he eased the door open and looked inside. There was one single brown letter sized envelope inside. He studied the interior of the box for several seconds before reaching in to remove it. Now that he was holding it he had to be concerned that it might be a letter bomb. How could he have existed all those years having to deal with this kind of fear every moment?

He ran his finger over the envelope carefully before slipping his thumb under the flap and unsealing it. It came open rather easily, indicating it hadn't been sealed very long ago. Inside was a single piece of white paper with two handwritten lines on it:

I'm at the Lafitte House
if you want to talk.

It was signed: *E.P.*

He folded the note and put it back in the envelope. As he turned to go back to the house, he swiped at the red flag to put it back down. As it came down it made a connection with a wire and a puff of smoke leaped into the air. Sangster took one step away from the box and watched the smoke rise and dissipate. Primble's sense of humor. He just wanted to show Sangster that he could be dead at that moment.

Instead of going back to his house he walked across to Burke's.

FOUR

"What are you going to do?" Burke asked.

"I'll have to handle it, somehow," Sangster said.

"You think he's here to kill you?"

"I think he was here to get me back," Sangster said. "Failing that, he'll have me killed."

"Not kill you himself?"

"No," Sangster said, "Primble doesn't kill. He has others do that for him."

"Like you?"

"Yes," Sangster said, "like me...at one time."

They were seated in Burke's kitchen, each with a Blackened Voodoo beer bottle in front of them. It was early, but they both thought the occasion called for it.

"He said he had guns with him," Burke said.

"I believe him."

"How many do you suppose?"

"At least two."

"And you plan on takin' them out?"

"Not if I can help it."

Burke leaned back and regarded his friend across the table.

"You said you don't kill for a livin' anymore."

"That's right."

"How about to survive?" Burke asked. "Could you kill then?"

Sangster stared at his beer bottle.

"I don't know, Burke," he said. "Are you a religious man?"

"No," Burke said, "not in any way you'd understand."

"Do you believe men have souls?" Sangster asked. "Souls that tell them what's right and what's wrong? Souls that make them feel compassion?"

"You're confusing a soul with a conscience, son," Burke said. "I know you told me you woke up three years ago and discovered you had both, but maybe it was just one."

"Which one?"

"That's for you to figure out. If you decide it's a soul, then you might not want to put any black marks on it. But if you decide it's a conscience—well, you can kill and still have a conscience."

"Am I kidding myself, Burke?" Sangster asked. "A hitman is all I've ever been. Can I be a hitman who won't kill?"

"A hitman is what you used to be, son," Burke said. "Just like a cop is what I used to be."

"You're still a cop, you old coot," Sangster said. "You've told me that a hundred times."

"Have I?" Burke asked. "Then who is the one kiddin' themselves?"

FIVE

Bourbon Street at midnight was a world unto itself.

The club doors were wide open, scantily-clad girls stood in windows and doorways, enticing men to come inside. One girl was riding on a swing, in and out of the window of a gentlemen's club. There were frozen Margarita bars on almost every corner, and almost every storefront—T-shirt shop, club, restaurant—and alcove had an ATM machine.

Sangster loved Bourbon Street, but tonight he could hear the music and voices floating on the air the two blocks to Chartres Street, where he was entering a small club just off of Jackson Square. He wore a pair of black cotton trousers, black T-shirt and a charcoal grey sport coat.

Sangster only came to the French Quarter a few times each month, sometimes during the day to prowl the used bookstores, other times late at night like this to hear the music. He had discovered the small Club Celestine—a distinctly Creole name—only a few months earlier, and this was his third time there.

Sangster was not a seafood lover, so he usually ordered either jambalaya or etouffe, both with chicken. Crawfish was something he had never even considered tasting and had never understood people's obsession with shrimp or crab legs.

He placed his order for jambalaya this time and an ice cold bottle of Abita, and settled back to enjoy the music which, tonight, was a Zydeco band.

"You came back," a woman's voice said.

He turned his head and looked up at her. She was tall, dark-haired and slender, probably thirty-three or thirty-four. Her green dress left her shoulders bare and the hem hit just above her knees. Certainly not risqué, but there was enough bare skin to be interesting. She had a long upper lip that kept her from being beautiful, but he doubted she ever got any complaints. The overall effect was extremely attractive.

She had spoken to him the last time he was there and, rather than be rude, he had bought her a drink. But he'd left the club alone that night, with the vague feeling she'd been disappointed. It wasn't that he didn't find her appealing—he certainly did—but years of killing people had left him ill-equipped to deal with the living, especially women. He could seduce a woman if his intent was to kill her or to use her to get to someone else, but in the real world he was rather inept at the dance that men and women took part in.

"I was sitting over there alone when I saw you come in," she said. "May I join you?"

"I, uh, already ordered," he said.

"So have I," she said, "but they can bring my plate over here. May I?"

He didn't know how to refuse, so he finally just said, "Sure."

"I'll get my drink."

As she hurried back to her table to pick up what looked like a martini, he thought back to how his day had started with Primble appearing on his doorstep. Having turned his ex-employer away he probably should have remained on Algiers for the evening, but he had already planned this trip into the Quarter and didn't want to let the man be the cause of his changing his plans. Besides, he didn't think Primble's men would come after him—at least not so soon. His former "handler" would at least want to wait a few days to see if Sangster would call him. (Primble called himself a "Handler." Sangster had always thought of him as more of a "Manager" or "Agent.")

The woman returned with her drink and sat down. Sangster stared across the table at her, trying to dredge up her name, which he was sure she had told him last time.

"You don't remember my name do you?" she asked.

Sangster had an excellent memory. It had served him well for years, freeing him from having to write anything down, like names, addresses or instructions.

"Of course I do."

"Well," she said, "I won't make a liar out of you by asking you to tell me what it is. Your name, on the other hand—well, you never told me your name last time, did you?"

"No, I didn't."

She raised her eyebrows, as if to say, "What about this time?"

"Stark," he told her, because he had never killed anyone while using that name and it was on the driver's license in his pocket. "Richard Stark."

"Stark?"

"Is there something wrong with that name?"

"No, no," she said, "it's a good name, strong, masculine, but not too testosterone fueled. I like it."

"I'm glad."

When the waiter came over, the woman said, "Could you bring my order over here, please? The gentleman was nice enough to ask me to join him."

"Yes, Miss."

When he walked away she looked up at the small stage, where the group was beginning to assemble.

"Do you like Zydeco?" she asked.

"Yes," he said, "quite a bit."

"So do I."

"Quite a coincidence that we're here again on the same night."

She sipped her drink and eyed him over the rim of the glass. "It's not really such a coincidence."

"No?" He wondered if she was going to tell him something he didn't want to know.

She shook her head. "Uh-uh. I come here almost every night."

"I see."

"So any time you come here, you'll probably see me."

"There are bigger and better clubs in the Quarter," he said. "Restaurants that serve better food. Why this one?"

"I happen to own a small piece of this one."

"Oh."

"So tell me, what are the better clubs with better food?"

"I put my foot in my mouth. Sorry."

"That's all right," she said, with a smile. "After all, you're here. You must like the music and the food."

"I do," Sangster said, "but mostly I like the size."

"Yes," she said, "it is...manageable."

That was a good word for it, Sangster thought. The club was manageable. He was able to enjoy his food, the music and see everyone in the room. The other larger, more crowded clubs and restaurants offered too much possibility of danger.

The waiter reappeared carrying their plates, and they leaned back to allow him to set them down. He noticed that the lady had ordered shrimp creole. He could smell the spices across the table. But his own jambalaya looked more appetizing to him.

The group began to play, making conversation impossible, so they ate and enjoyed the music together.

SIX

Sangster found himself laughing.

He hadn't laughed in a very long time. They finished their dinner, had some dessert, more drinks, more music, and he was laughing.

Her name was Lily. He remembered while they were eating. He saved it, though. Wouldn't say it until later, when she was convinced he had forgotten. It was then Sangster realized he was not only laughing, he was being playful.

He thought it was very unlike him, but then decided it was just unlike the man he used to be. He didn't know if it was unlike Sangster, because he still wasn't sure what Sangster was like.

They were finishing up their desserts when the group took a break.

"Do you want to meet them?" she asked.

"Why?"

"Because as part owner I can have them come to the table."

"No," he said, "that's okay."

"Why not?"

"I enjoy the music," he said. "I don't enjoy making small talk."

"Isn't that what we're doing?" she asked. "Making small talk?"

"I don't know what we're doing," he admitted.

She studied him for a moment, then said, "You don't, do you?"

He shrugged.

"You're a rare man, you know?"

"How so?"

"Well, for one thing, you don't seem to have an ego."

"And for another?"

"You seem to be fairly honest," she said. "Unless this shy boy thing of yours is an act?"

"'Shy boy?'"

"Don't be ashamed," she said. "I'm finding it...refreshing. And genuine. If you turn out to be a player I'm going to be very disappointed."

"A 'player.'" These were terms that had never before been used to describe him. He had been a player in his own business for many years, but not in the way she meant.

"I get the feeling you're a man out of time," Lily said. "Like...you were just thawed out yesterday. Were you?"

"Was I what?"

"Thawed out?"

He took a sip of his coffee and said, "Not yesterday."

Sangster stayed for another set, some more coffee rather than another beer. Lily did the same, eschewing another martini for coffee.

When the band broke for the night to a smattering of appreciative applause from those who had remained for the final set, Sangster said, "I have to go."

"Really?" she asked.

"Yes," he said, "I have to get back."

"Wife?"

"No."

"Roommate?"

"No wife," he said, "no roommate."

"Then what's the hurry?"

"I came for the music," he said. "The music is done."

"Stay for another reason," she said, looking him directly in the eye. "I live upstairs."

He stared across the table at her. In truth, she had become more and more appealing as the night went on, especially that overly long upper lip.

But he couldn't stay. He'd been avoiding personal conflict for three years. Getting involved with a woman was inviting conflict. He had let his guard down with Burke, but that had worked out. What were the chances it would happen again?

"Okay, then," she said, sitting back. "We don't close for another hour or so. Let me know if you change your mind."

"I'll get the check—" he said, raising his arm for the waiter.

"Forget it," she said. "On me."

"Why would you do that?"

She grinned and said, "I'm a sucker for men who play hard to get."

He stood up and said, "I'm not playing."

"Yeah," she said, "I know."

"Good-night, Lily." It was the first time he let her know he remembered her name.

He walked to the front door, stopped and looked through the glass. His eyes scanned the street, the shadows across the way, the shapes in them.

He turned and walked back to Lily's table.

"I changed my mind."

SEVEN

He woke the next morning to the smell of ham.

He looked around at the brick walls and high ceiling. The bed was king-sized, with satin sheets smooth on his naked skin.

Sitting up in bed he remembered coming up the stairs to the apartment with Lily after she closed the restaurant. They had some drinks, but he had never intended for them to go to bed. He knew that Primble's two men were across the street from the restaurant, watching him. They probably had no intention of doing anything then and there, but it annoyed him that they'd been able to follow him there without him knowing it. He needed some time to think. So going upstairs with Lily was only supposed to kill time—say, an hour or two.

But one thing led to another...

"Breakfast!" she yelled from the kitchen.

"Coming."

He stood up, looked around for his clothes, found that she had laid out a dressing gown for him. Also silk. He put it on and went in search of the kitchen.

Except for the bedroom, the rest of the apartment was all one room. He crossed the living room part to the kitchen, where she had breakfast already on the table.

"Ham-'n-eggs?" he asked.

"Not quite," she said. "Have you been to Brennan's?"

"I haven't."

"Well, this is my take on their grilled ham steak royale."

He sat, looked down at the two poached eggs on top of the ham steak, covered in hollandaise sauce.

"I've added some spices to their recipe," she said, sitting across from him. "If they find out, they'll sue me, so I'm relying on your discretion."

"Of course."

She had prepared some English muffins, already buttered, coffee and Mimosas.

He used his knife, speared the eggs, ham and sauce and put it in his mouth.

"How is it?"

"It's great," he told her, truthfully.

"Good, I'm glad."

She was wearing a dressing gown similar to his, purple to his blue. He knew the body beneath the silk was sleek and smooth. Her nipples made little bumps against the fabric.

He ate some English muffin, washed it down with a sip of the Mimosa and then coffee.

"So tell me," she said, "what really made you change your mind last night? It certainly wasn't my beautiful eyes or charming smile."

"I decided," he said, "it was too good an opportunity to pass up."

"Well," she said, "you had me fooled."

"Oh? In what way?"

"I expected you to be a little...well, inept, sexually," she said. "I mean, you didn't seem to be too experienced at talking to women, so..."

"I hope your suspicions weren't right."

"Not at all," she said. "I was pleasantly surprised. You certainly know your way around a bed."

"Thank you, Ma'am."

"I guess it's just the dance beforehand where you need some help."

"I'm not so good with people," he said. Not live ones, anyway. Kind of hard to have experience with the living when most of his time had been spent putting people in the ground.

They chatted over breakfast. Actually, she talked and he listened. He discovered that she had been married twice, widowed twice, the combined inheritances making her a very rich woman.

"Seems to me," he said, "you could open a restaurant that would rival anything Emeril Lagasse has in this town."

"That's not what I want," she said. "I bought this building and opened the restaurant I wanted to open."

"You can certainly cook," he said, placing another bite into his mouth.

"I don't cook in the restaurant," she said. "Only cook for myself and for...special people."

They finished breakfast and he helped her clean the table. Standing close together at the sink the scent of her was heady, and he reached for her. She was naked beneath the silk.

"You don't usually have dessert after breakfast," she said, coming into his arms.

He slid his hands inside the dressing gown. Her skin as even smoother than the silk.

"We'll start something new," he told her.

They kissed, the two silk gowns slipping to the floor. Then she pushed away.

"Not here," she said. "Why do you think I have such a big bed?"

She took hold of his hardening penis and led him across the loft into the bedroom.

EIGHT

Later, as they lay entwined together on the bed, she said, "I've done all the talking, Stark."

"Uh-huh."

"Are you ready to do some?"

"Mmm, not yet."

"Okay." She snuggled closer to him. "I won't push. It'll mean more when you finally tell me about yourself because you want to."

"You're an unusual woman," he said.

"Yes," she said, "I am."

When she fell asleep he slipped from the bed, found his clothes and got dressed. He walked to the windows that overlooked Chartres Street. They were virtually floor to ceiling. Just outside was a gallery that ran the width of the building. He didn't get closer, though. He didn't want to be seen, if anyone was watching.

There was a corner window, though, from where he could see the street. People were strolling, but no one seemed to be watching the building. Maybe they gave up, figured they'd missed him. And maybe they were never there at all. After all, he was out if practice.

He wrote a note to Lily and left the apartment. By trial and error he finally found a back way out of the building, through the restaurant's kitchen.

He'd parked his car on St. Peters Street. He was so aware of everyone he passed on the street as he made his way to it. If Primble's men had really wanted him, they probably could have had him. He was unarmed. There wasn't much he could do if they came at him with guns. But he made it to the car without incident. Using the ferry, he'd be back in Algiers in fifteen minutes.

"So you think they were watchin' you?" Burke asked, a half hour later.

He had come over to Sangster's house when he saw that his friend was home, having been worried when he didn't return the night before.

"I don't know," Sangster said. "Maybe I was imagining things. It's been three years since I had to rely on those senses."

"They don't go away," Burke said. "You'll just need to sharpen them up a little."

"I don't want to sharpen them," Sangster said. "That would be taking a step backwards."

"Well, you may not have a choice, if what you say about this Primble guy is true," the ex-Orleans Parish Sheriff said.

"The Primble I knew wouldn't come all this way to find me, and then let me go," Sangster said. "But maybe he's changed."

"Do you really believe that?"

"No."

They were sitting on Sangster's porch, each with a Blackened Voodoo in their hand.

Algiers was a large community in New Orleans' 15th ward, across from the French Quarter on the West Bank of the Mississippi. It was the home to numerous churches and "dens"—warehouses—of many of the New Orleans' carnival crews.

But it was also cut up into many smaller neighborhoods. The one Sangster had chosen to live in was called Algiers Point, made up of bars, restaurants, coffee shops and various other businesses, as well as historical homes, many of which dated back to before the Civil War. Sangster's house, however, was one of many which had been built following the 1885 fire which had destroyed hundreds of buildings in the area.

As for Katrina, Algiers had luckily managed to avoid getting flooded.

Sangster had hoped against hope that no one would manage to find him there. He hadn't even asked Primble how he'd done it, but it occurred to him now that it was something he needed to find out.

"Sangster!"

The ex-assassin started, became aware that Burke had said his name several times.

"Yeah, what?"

"Where did you go?"

"Just thinking."

"About what you're gonna do?"

"About what I *should* do," Sangster said. "Unfortunately, I haven't really decided what I'm going to do, yet"

"And when do you think you'll do that?" Burke asked him.

Sangster held up his now empty beer bottle and said, "Maybe after a few more of these."

"Allow me," Burke said, and went into Sangster's house to retrieve a few more bottles from the fridge.

Sangster stared out at the empty street in front of his house. There had to be some way for him to handle this without picking up a gun, without killing anyone.

There had to be.

Primble sat in an antique wicker chair in his room at the Jean Lafitte House in the French Quarter, holding a snifter of brandy. He hated siccing his two dogs—Silk

Guiliano and Jimmy O'Malley—onto Sangster, who was the best killer he'd ever represented. But the man was three years out of practice, so maybe the two would be able to take him. They certainly would not have been able to take the man Sangster used to be.

And if Sangster managed to kill Guiliano and O'Malley, maybe that would once again wet his appetite for murder, which used to be unquenchable. Sangster had always been good because he enjoyed the killing. It was more than a job he did for money. It was a way of life for him. That was something Primble had always liked—and feared, a little—about Sangster.

Primble was sure he only needed to awaken those old feelings in the hitman, and he would come back to the fold.

NINE

It was an old house, and after living there three years, Sangster had every creak memorized. That's how he knew right where the assassin was from the moment he stepped up onto the porch.

He sat in the dark, in the living room, waiting. At one time he would have been holding a gun in his hand, but on this night instead of a Colt Woodsman or a Glock, he was holding a Louisville Slugger.

Whoever the mechanic was, he stood at a window now, sliding it open as gently as he could. Unfortunately for him, the sound of the window was very familiar to Sangster who, even in the dark, was able to pinpoint it and position himself.

Entering from outside, the hitter had no night vision inside the room. That was a mistake. He should have taken steps to make sure he'd be able to see when he entered the house. Having been inside the entire time, not having to deal with moonlight, Sangster could see very well as first a leg came through the window, then a shoulder and then a gun. Another mistake. The man should have led with the gun first. Where was Primble getting these guys?

Sangster's first swing knocked the gun from the hitter's hand. It flew across the room into the darkness and landed with a few clatters and a thud.

The man yelled, staggered as his other foot came in through the window. Sangster picked a knee and let fly with the bat. There was a satisfying popping sound accompanied by a nice tremor up through the bat and into his arms. It was like hitting a home run.

Primble's man screamed and went down, holding onto his knee with both hands. Sangster took a moment to turn on a nearby lamp, then moved it so it shone into the man's eyes, illuminating his face.

"Quiet down!" Sangster said.

"Oh, man!" the guy shouted. "Aw, my knee!"

"If you don't shut up, I'll pop the other one."

"What the hell, man?" the guy moaned.

"Okay," Sangster said, and pulled the bat back for another swing.

"No, wait!" the man screamed, holding his hands out in front of him.

"What?"

"I'll—I'll try to q-quiet down."

Sangster relaxed, letting the bat come back down. He pressed the barrel of the bat against the man's chest to get his attention again, prodded him a bit.

"Name?" he said.

"O—O'Malley," the man said. "Jimmy O'Malley."

"You work for Primble." That wasn't so much a question as it was a statement.

"Y-yes."

O'Malley's face was all screwed up in pain, but while one hand was clutching his knee the other one was moving down his leg.

"You pull that gun from your ankle holster and I'll split your head like a watermelon."

O'Malley's hand came away as if the gun was scalding. Sangster retrieved the little .22 and sent it sailing in the same direction as the other gun, into the darkness.

"How many of you are here?"

"T-two."

"The other one outside?"

"No."

"What's the other one's name?"

"Guiliano," the injured man said, "Silk Guiliano."

"Silk?" Sangster asked. "Is that his real name?"

"Shit, man, I dunno," O'Malley whined.

Sangster put pressure on the bat, still pressing it into the man's chest, then patted him down. No third gun, no wallet. All he found was a King of Spades in the man's pocket.

"What's this?"

"W-we cut for you."

"What?"

"We cut the cards to see who would try you first," O'Malley said. "I—I won."

Sangster placed the barrel of the bat beneath the man's chin and said, "No, Jimmy, I think you lost."

The next morning Ed Primble met Silk Guiliano at Café Du Mond for a breakfast of coffee and beignets. Primble was already present, working on his second cup of coffee. There was a fine mist of powder on the lapels of his dark suit. Normally fastidious about his appearance, he didn't seem to mind.

"He didn't come back," Silk said, sitting opposite Primble.

"He's probably dead."

"Then I win."

Primble licked three of his fingers, then waggled one of them at the younger man.

"Not until you've killed him," he said, chewing. "That was the wager."

"But...he can't win if he's dead."

"And neither can you," Primble said. "You'll have to take your shot, Silk. That's the only way you'll win...or lose, clearly and fairly."

A waitress came over. Silk asked for coffee and then waved her off when she started to ask if he wanted a beignet. Primble, however, stopped her and asked her to bring him still another order of the delicious powdered pastries.

"How can you come to New Orleans and not have a beignet from Café Du Mond?" he asked.

"I'm not hungry."

"Could that be because you're a little nervous?"

"I'm a lot nervous, Primble," Silk said. "I'm not a fool. I know Sangster was your best once."

"He was the very best I ever saw," Primble said.

"Well then, it's only natural that I'd be...concerned."

"Not...scared?"

"No, not scared. Jimmy was good, though. If Sangster took him out, then he's still got skills."

"Of course he's got skills," Primble said, "which is more than I could say for Jimmy O'Malley."

"You didn't think Jimmy was good?"

Primble made a face.

"Second rate, at best."

"And me?"

"You?" Primble asked. He sat back then, fell silent as the waitress set his new treat in front of him.

"Sure you won't have a bite?" he asked Silk.

"Answer my question, Primble," Silk said. "Do you think I'm second rate...or first?"

Primble took a bite of the beignet, sending a whole new curtain of powder down upon himself.

"That, dear boy," he said, "remains to be seen."

TEN

Sangster did not want to give Primble or his second man time to adjust to missing Jimmy O'Malley, so he caught the first ferry in the morning to the Quarter. He refused Burke's offer of a gun, and also the old man's offer to go with him.

"If I don't come back, everything in the house is yours."

"Who you kiddin'. You ain't got nothin' in that house."

"There's good beer in the fridge."

"That I'll take."

The two men shook hands at the dock.

Once he was in the Quarter he knew where Primble was staying, but not where Silk Guiliano was staying. That meant Primble had to tell him where Guiliano was, even if he didn't want to.

He arrived outside the Lafitte House early enough to catch Primble coming out. He followed the man to Café Du Mond, watched him consume four beignets, two before another man joined him and two after. Sangster assumed this was Silk Guiliano.

He watched while the two men spoke. Primble remained calm, Guiliano became agitated. Sangster knew this because the man did not eat a beignet. He had to be otherwise occupied to be able to resist eating just one.

When the two men left at the same time, Sangster followed Guiliano.

Guiliano seemed to wander the Quarter aimlessly. Sangster remained half a block behind him and across the street, reasonably certain he had gone unnoticed. He trailed the man for a couple of hours. During that time there were any number of locations that would have lent themselves to murder. One in particular was when the man ducked down Pirate's Alley which, at that time of the day, was not very busy. It would have been relatively easy to take the man right in front of The Faulkner House, drag him into the shadows of St. Louis Cathedral and kill him—if he had been so inclined.

He was not.

After two and a half hours, Guiliano finally stopped at a restaurant called Remoulade's on Bourbon Street. Sangster knew the place, had eaten there many times. He crossed the street and looked in the window. Since Guiliano worked for Primble, he halfway expected the man to be gone, perhaps out the back door. Instead, Guiliano had been seated at a table away from the few other diners in the place.

Sangster decided this was as good a place and time as any...

"Silk Guiliano?"

The man looked up, frowned.

"Who's asking?"

"I think you know."

Silk's eyes widened.

"Sangster?"

"That's right. Mind if I sit?"

Before Silk could say a word, Sangster was seated across from him.

"I think we need to talk."

"About what?"

"Your friend O'Malley. He gave you up."

"He's not my friend."

"Colleague, then."

"Whatever."

Sangster looked around. The waitress who was approaching was unfamiliar to him. That was good.

"Have you ordered yet? I'd suggest a Po' Boy. They do them really well, here."

"I...was just gonna have a drink."

"Good. I'll join you. A beer all right?"

"Fine."

As the waitress reached them Sangster said, "Two Abitas, please."

"Yessir."

"You'll like it. It's a good beer."

"What do you want, Sangster?"

"I want to save your life."

"*Save* my life?" Guiliano asked "Or take it?"

"Do you want me to take it?"

"I thought you told Primble you don't kill anymore."

Sangster smiled. The man had just admitted to working for Primble. That was on Primble's list of things not to do.

"That's right, I don't."

"Then what do I have to fear?"

"I don't know."

The waitress came with two sweating bottles of Abita.

"Ahh," Sangster said, after downing a good sized swallow.

Guiliano lifted his bottle to his mouth, preparing to take a drink. Moving quickly Sangster drove the heel of his hand into the bottom of the bottle, driving it into the other man's mouth. Teeth broke, blood spurted and

Guiliano screamed. He dropped the bottle and pressed his hands against his mouth.

Sangster got to his feet, took Guiliano by the shoulders and threw him to the floor, chair and all.

"You're not good enough, Silk," he hissed into the bleeding man's ear before anyone could reach them. "Go home!"

Sangster was out the door as the waitress and another person reached Guiliano.

ELEVEN

When Edward Primble entered his suite at the Lafitte House he stopped short. His stomach muscles tensed as he noticed Sangster sitting in the large wicker chair at the far end of the room. He half expected a bullet to rip through his chest, but Sangster was sitting very calmly, his left ankle resting on his right thigh.

"How did you get in here?" Primble asked.

"Easy," Sangster said. "I just asked downstairs what the most expensive suite was. Then I asked if it was available. When they said no, I knew it was yours."

"Smart," Primble said. He'd been inching toward a small table near the door with one drawer in it. Sangster pretended not to notice. Finally, Primble lunged, opened the drawer and took out a handgun. It was small, a silver .32 that held five shots. He pointed it at Sangster and grinned.

"Now what?" he asked.

"It would work better with these." Sangster tossed all five bullets onto the floor between them. Primble paled as they struck the carpet, rolled and lay still.

"What do you want to bet I can get to you before you can get one of those loaded?"

Sangster was surprised Primble actually thought it over, but finally he tossed the gun onto the bed. He showed Sangster his empty hands.

"So," Primble said. "Have you come to kill me?"

"I told you, Ed," Sangster said. "I don't do that anymore."

"What about O'Malley?"

"He's not dead. He's in the hospital, but he's not dead."

"And Silk?"

"I suspect he's in the emergency room about now," Sangster said, "but not dead. He'll probably need some dental work, though. I expect you'll stand good for all their medical bills?"

"You did all this without killing them, and without a gun?" Primble asked.

"That's right."

Primble smiled.

"And you said you were retired."

"I am."

"Retired, but not rusty."

"Very rusty," Sangster said. "Luckily, the men you sent against me weren't very good."

"I didn't send them," Primble said. "They volunteered."

"You pay them, and you told them where I was."

"They're not being paid," Primble said.

"Oh, that's right," Sangster said, "there was a bet."

"The winner gets your old job."

"Which you've held open for three years hoping I'd come back?" Sangster asked.

"Of course."

"I'm flattered, Ed."

"Don't be," Primble said. "You're one of a kind, Sangster. A natural. I never saw anyone take to it the way you did. No conscience and no soul. The perfect killing machine."

"Not anymore."

"Why?" Primble asked. "Just tell me why?"

"I woke up one morning, and there they were," Sangster said. "My soul, my conscience."

"Just like that?"

"Just like that."

Primble frowned.

"I've lost it, Ed. It's gone. I can't do it anymore."

"Maybe if you...tried?"

"What about today?" Sangster asked. "Your O'Malley and Silk. If it was in me—anywhere in me anymore—don't you think I would have killed them? And you?"

"Well, them maybe," Primble said, "but not me. We go back a long ways, Sangster."

"Were we friends, Ed?" Sangster asked. "Were we ever friends?"

"Sure we were. We were—"

"When's my birthday?"

Primble didn't answer.

"Where am I from originally?"

No answer.

"What's my first name?"

"Okay," Primble said, "so I sluff off the personal details. They never mattered, Sangster. What mattered was you did the job. Every time. No hitches."

"Read my lips, Ed," Sangster said. "Not anymore."

He got up from the chair and Primble tensed, his eyes going to the gun on the bed, then the bullets on the floor. Sangster started for the door, stopped next to Primble, who was several inches shorter than he was. He leaned down to speak into the smaller man's ear.

"Don't send those two after me again, Ed. Don't send anyone else after me. Or we might have to really test out your theory that it's still in me."

"Sangster—"

"Shhh," Sangster said. "Don't say anything else. There's nothing else to say. The next time I see you, Ed, I'll kill you."

"But...you just said you can't—"

"Assassinate," Sangster said, "I don't—can't—assassinate anymore. Maybe, though—just maybe—I can still kill in self-defense."

He patted Primble on the shoulder—felt the man start—and then went out the door.

Halfway back to Algiers, he realized he hadn't asked Primble how he'd found him.

Crap.

"You should have killed him," Burke said. "You should have killed all of them."

They were sitting at a wooden table outside an Algiers sandwich shop with a Po' Boy and an Abita each. They had brought a chessboard with them, but had not yet started a game. It was the day after Sangster had gone to the Quarter to deal with Guiliano and Ed Primble.

"Burke," Sangster said, his tone reproachful, "I thought you didn't approve of my old ways."

"I don't," Burke said. "This would have been your new way. Killing Primble and his two dogs would have been self- defense."

As far as Sangster knew, O'Malley and Guiliano were still in the hospital. He hoped Primble had left.

"Couldn't do it, Burke."

"Why not?"

"I think," Sangster said, hesitantly, "it would have cost me my soul."

"So, you think it would have been a sin?" Burke said, with a shrug. "Go to confession."

"I'm not Catholic," Sangster said. "Besides, I don't know that this is anything religious."

"Were you raised in any religion, Sangster?"

"I was raised in foster homes," Sangster said. "Nobody worried about religion. They worried about the check they got from the state."

Burke nodded.

"I left the last one when I was fifteen. I don't believe in any organized religion, Burke. I'm not even sure I believe in God."

"But you say you have a soul."

"I don't know what else to call it," Sangster said. "You said conscience. Maybe that's it. I don't know. I just know that I think if I kill again, I'll lose it. I'll go back...to the way I was."

"I get it," Burke said. "I still think maybe you should talk to the priest or a rabbi or somebody...but I get it."

They sat in silence for a few moments, eating and contemplating their first moves.

"So you think this is it?" Burke asked, then. "It's finished?"

"I hope so," Sangster said. "If it's not, I'll have to leave."

"So when will we know for sure?"

"Soon," Sangster said. "We'll know soon."

Burke reached out and moved his Queen's Pawn to Queen's Four.

"I hope you're right," he said.

Sangster moved his Black Rook to the corresponding square and said, "I hope so, too, Burke. I really hope so, too."

TWELVE

The next few days were uneventful.

Sangster checked with the hospital. Neither hitter was there, neither had ever been registered as a patient.

He checked sat the Lafitte House and found that Primble had checked out.

Nobody took a shot at him, and his mailbox didn't blow up.

Hopefully, he had handled the situation the right way.

After several more days Sangster decided to return to the French Quarter. He took the ferry at seven p.m., drove to St. Peters Street, around the corner from Chartres and walked to the Club Celestine. When he reached the front door, he found it locked. The hours were posted on the door, and according to them, the club should have been open. He peered in through the glass front door, saw a man behind the bar and knocked. The man looked up, waved him off, and went back to what he was doing. He recognized the man as having been behind the bar the last night he was there, so he knocked again, insistently, this time.

Annoyed, the bartender came around the bar and approached the door.

"We're not open!" the bartender said.

"Open the door," Sangster said. "I want to talk to you."

The man shook his head.

"It's about your boss, Lily."

The man's eyes widened. He thought a moment, then reluctantly unlocked the door, but opened it only a crack. He was a few inches shorter than Sangster's six feet, younger—in his twenties—and in good shape. He probably did well with female patrons.

"Look at me," Sangster said to him. "Do you remember me?"

The man studied him for a moment, then brightened.

"Hey, yeah, yeah," he said, "you were here the other night."

"Right," Sangster said, "I was sitting with Lily."

"Yeah, I remember now," the man said. "You were still here with her when I left."

"Right. Is she in?"

"Um..."

"Or is she home? Upstairs?"

"Um..."

"Why are you closed?" Sangster asked, figuring maybe that was an easier question. He pointed to the hours on the door.

"Um, Mister," the bartender said, "maybe you ain't heard, but Lily...she's dead."

"What?"

"Yeah," the man said, "she got killed a couple of nights ago."

"A couple of nights?" Sangster asked. "How many, exactly?"

"Um...well, I guess it was three."

"You guess?"

"Three," the man said. "It was three."

"Where did it happen?"

"Upstairs."

"How?"

"Somebody broke in and killed her."

"How?"

"That I don't know," he said. "Look, I just work here."

"Did she have any partners?"

"Nope."

"But she told me owned a piece of this place."

"She did," the bartender said. "A big piece. A hundred percent."

Sangster passed his hand over his mouth, thinking. Coincidence? Couldn't be. He must have been right about Primble's men being across the street from the club, in the shadows. They must have seen him with Lily, maybe thought they were a couple.

"Look," he said, "I'd like to get a look upstairs."

"What for?"

"I'm curious," Sangster said. "Anybody else here?"

"No, just me. I'm just...I don't know, I don't know what else to do but work, you know?"

"I know," Sangster said, putting his hand in his pocket. "Look, it's worth a hundred bucks to me. I just want to have a look."

"There's a police seal on the door."

"I can get around that."

"You ain't gonna steal anything, are you?"

"I'm not here to steal," Sangster said. "I'd like to see if I can figure out what happened."

"Why don't you talk to the cops?"

"I don't like cops."

The man frowned at him.

"You ain't a cop, are you? Maybe tryin' to trick me?"

"I'm not a cop." Sangster showed him the hundred dollar bill. "If I was, I wouldn't be giving you this."

He could have gone to the back door and let himself in, but at the time he thought this was simpler.

The bartender eyed the Benjamin for a second, then snatched it from Sangster's hand before he could change his mind.

"You know the way?" he asked.

THIRTEEN

He wasn't delicate about it. All it took was the edge of a key to break the seal on the yellow police tape. He entered and closed the door behind him. He didn't think he could trust the bartender not to call someone, maybe even the police, so he moved about the loft quickly.

The place looked as if it had been tossed. He didn't know if the police could be blamed for that or if Lily had fought with her attacker. If she did, then she must have struggled across the length of the room. In the bedroom, he found the blood. There was enough of it to make him think she'd been stabbed or slashed. Maybe her throat had been cut. There was some arterial spray on the walls and ceiling. She obviously had not been shot. This was done with a blade.

Now the question was, why? Was this a coincidence? Or a message from Primble? If it was a message then her death was his fault. He had obviously not handled the situation correctly. He wasn't ready to agree with Burke that he should have killed all three men, but he was ready to admit he should have come up with something better.

But he needed to know for sure.

If Primble had his boys do it he would have wanted Sangster to know. Maybe he had them leave a message.

He went through the entire place as thoroughly and as quickly as he could. The problem was the police had already been through it, so if there had been a message, maybe they had already found it but didn't know what it meant.

Sangster went to the front window and looked out. Then he opened the window and climbed out onto the gallery. From there he could look right down to the street. If the cops were going to come they'd be there any min—and there they were. His timing was right on the money.

He had two choices: run out the back before they got up there or stay and play it straight with them. Even if they took him in, questioned him and checked his prints, they'd find nothing because he had never been fingerprinted. And maybe he'd discover if they had taken something out of the apartment that meant nothing to them, but would mean something to him.

He decided to play it straight. After all, he was innocent. And didn't they say the innocent had nothing to fear?

He was going to put that to the test.

FOURTEEN

Sangster originally planned to be sitting on the sofa when the cops came in, but decided that would make him look too...well, cool. Too much like he was expecting them. So he changed his mind just in time, and as two detectives entered the room he was standing. He turned and froze, staring at them.

"Just stand still, sir," one of them said. Neither man had his gun out, which was a good sign.

"What's—what's going on?" Sangster asked.

"That's what we'd like to know," the other one said. He was younger, slimmer, dressed a little more informal—meaning he wasn't wearing a tie. He also had an expensive haircut and shoes to match. The first one was dressed more the way Sangster remembered cops did.

"You broke a police seal getting in here, sir," the first man said. "Would you like to explain that?"

"Um, sure."

"But first," the second man said, "I'd like to frisk you—if you don't mind?"

"Frisk me? Oh, you mean...oh, I don't have a weapon," Sangster said.

"Do you mind if we check?" the first man asked.

"Not at all," Sangster said. "What do I do, raise my hands?" He put his hands in the air.

"That's not necessary, sir," the first man said. "Just extend them out from your sides while my partner checks you."

"Sure."

He did as he was told and the younger detective frisked him.

"My name is Detective Telemaco," the older man said, "and that's my partner, Detective Williams."

"How do you do?"

"And your name?"

Sangster had no choice. He had an ID on him with a phony name—one of several he maintained for emergencies.

"Stark."

"You got ID.?"

"My wallet's in my pants pocket."

Williams dipped in and came out with it. He opened it, found the license.

"Richard Stark," Williams said. He looked at Sangster.

"That's my name."

"Okay, Richard, here ya go," Williams said, handing him back his wallet. "You can put your hands down." Williams looked at Telemaco. "He's clean."

Williams walked back to stand next to his partner.

"Mr. Stark, this is a crime scene. You care to tell us what you're doing here?"

"I came here to see Lily," Sangster said. "The bartender downstairs told me she was dead. I—I couldn't believe it."

"Why not?" Telemaco asked.

"Well, she seemed...she was so alive when I saw her last week." Sangster had heard people say something like that countless times. Just because somebody was alive the last time you saw them, why does that make it impossible that they're now dead? Still, he thought the comment was fitting here for the character he was portraying.

"Last week? Is that the last time you saw her?" Williams asked.

"That's right."

"What was the occasion?" Telemaco asked.

"I just came in to hear some music. We met and hit it off."

"Did you spend the night together?"

Sangster had the feeling they were asking questions they already knew the answers to. They wanted to see if he would lie.

"Yes, we did."

"Why don't we have a seat?" Telemaco said. "We're going to be here a while."

FIFTEEN

Sangster looked behind him, backed up to the sofa and sat. Contrary to the suggestion, the two detectives remained standing. It gave them an advantage—they were looking down at him, and he had to look up.

"Was that the first time you had ever spent the night?" the older detective asked.

"Yes, it was."

Sangster wondered why they weren't taking him to the police station to interrogate him. After all, they had found him at the scene of the murder having broken the police seal.

Williams had been holding something in his hands that Sangster had assumed was a clipboard. Now he brought it up and turned it on, revealing it to be a tablet. He began to take notes.

"And was that the first time you'd met?"

"No," Sangster said, "we met a few weeks before, when I first came to the club."

"So you weren't a regular patron of the club?" Telemaco seemed to have taken over the questioning.

"No."

"Why not?"

Sangster decided to stick to his decision to be honest.

"I live over in Algiers Point."

"Still," Telemaco said, "it's only a fifteen or twenty minute ride by ferry."

"True," Sangster said. "I do come to the Quarter often, but sometimes, it's to go to bookstores."

"Bookstores?" Williams asked.

"That's right."

"You don't look like the type," the younger detective said.

"What type is that...sir?"

"A bookworm."

"I don't know that I'd call myself a bookworm," Sangster said. "I just like to read."

"Don't you have one of those...what do they call 'em...Kindling or Crook things?" Telemaco asked.

"Kindle or Nook," his partner said, looking up from his tablet.

"I prefer to hold a real book in my hands."

Telemaco shrugged, and appeared ready to give the floor back to his partner. But before either could speak Sangster did.

"There's so much blood in the bedroom. Is that where..."

Neither detective seemed inclined to make things easy for him.

"...she was killed?" he finished.

"Yes," Telemaco said.

"But...how?"

"Somebody cut her up pretty bad," Telemaco said. "We're not sure what they used, but it definitely had a sharp edge."

"That's terrible."

"So, tell me," Telemaco said, "why was it so important to come up here that you'd give the bartender a hundred bucks?"

"Yeah," Williams said, "what were you looking for?"

"I just...couldn't believe that she was dead. The bartender couldn't—or wouldn't—tell me how she died, so I just thought I'd come up and, well, look around."

"Not looking for anything in particular," Telemaco said.

"No," Sangster said, "why, did you find something?"

"Like what?" Williams asked.

The two detectives had subtly moved further apart. Sangster figured they were about to start sharing the interrogation, so that he'd have to move his head back and forth between them, like it was some sort of verbal tennis match. Williams may have been younger, but Sangster had a feeling these two had been partners for a long time.

"I'm sure I don't know," Sangster said. "You were just asking me if I was looking for something. I just thought maybe you found something."

"Like what?" Telemaco asked.

"I don't know."

"You sure about that?" Williams asked.

"I'm sure I don't know what you're trying to get me to say." Sangster obliged them and turned his head to each as they spoke. Let them think their interrogation technique was succeeding.

"We're not trying to get you to say anything but the truth," Telemaco said.

"And I've told you the truth."

"Still bothers me that you came up here," Williams said.

"I'm sorry," Sangster said, "it was a spur of the moment decision. Wait a minute." He contrived to look as if something had just occurred to him. "Do you think—you don't think that I had something to—to do with this...do you?"

"I don't know," Telemaco said. He looked at his partner. "You think he did it?"

"Well," Williams said, "if he did, why'd he come back?"

"You know what they say," Telemaco said. "The killer always returns to the scene of the crime."

"Who says that?"

"I don't know," Telemaco said. "Somebody."

"Did you get that from some old movie?" Williams asked. "I'm telling you, Aaron, you need to update your references."

"The old ones are always the best."

"I'm sorry," Sangster said, "but...do you need anything else from me?"

"Oh," Telemaco said, "yeah, we do." He reached behind him, came out with cuffs dangling from his hand. "Slip these on for us, will you?"

"Handcuffs?" Sangster asked, looking alarmed. "What for?"

"You didn't think we were just going to let you walk after you broke our seal, did you?" Williams asked. "Our boss takes those seals very seriously."

"B-but...does this mean I'm under arrest?"

The two detectives exchanged a look, and Williams shrugged.

"Oh, I don't know," Telemaco said, stepping forward. "Why don't we see how they fit before we decide? Would you mind standing up?"

SIXTEEN

It was late afternoon when Sangster came walking out the front door of the police department building at 715 South Broad St. They'd been nice enough during four hours of interrogation to give him six cups of bad police department coffee. He headed directly for Café Du Mond to get that taste out of his mouth.

While seated with some excellent coffee and a couple of beignets, he went over the past four hours. He'd answered every question they'd thrown at him. He was sure he had given them nothing they could use against him. After all, he *was* an innocent man.

He thought about the woman, Lily. Was she dead because of him? Or was her murder a complete coincidence? He had found nothing in her apartment to answer those questions. The detectives hadn't told him about anything they'd found. All he had was his instincts, and they told him this was his fault. Lily had been killed because of what he'd done to Primble and his two men. He barely knew the woman, and yet she had paid the price for his inability to get the job done.

It wasn't right.

"Why do you have to leave?" Burke asked.

They were sitting on Sangster's porch having one last chess match. Next to Sangster was his suitcase. Just one. When he traveled now, he traveled light.

"They'll leave you alone, won't they?" Burke asked. "After this?"

"Maybe," Sangster said, "but I can't leave them alone, Burke."

"You're not even sure they killed her, Sangster."

"I know they did," he said. "I know Primble had it done."

"And do you know where Primble is now?"

"No," Sangster said, "but I made a call."

"And?"

"And soon I'll know."

"So where are you going now?"

Sangster continued to stare at the board.

"Yeah, okay," Burke said, "you can't tell me that. But tell me this."

"What?"

"Are you coming back?"

Sangster moved a Knight and looked up from the board.

"I don't know that, Burke."

"Okay, let me put it another way," the ex-lawman said, moving a Bishop. "If you live through this, will you be back?"

Sangster shrugged.

"What about the local cops?" Burke asked. "You think they're just gonna forget you, after finding you at their crime scene?"

"No," Sangster said, moving a Rook. "Even after hours of interrogation, no, I don't think they'll forget me."

"You didn't tell them where you really live, did you?" Burke asked.

"I had to. If they went looking for me and found out I lied, I'd shoot to the top of their suspect list."

"Okay," Burke said, moving his Queen. "Check. So what happens when they come out here to talk to you again, and find that you're gone?"

"Well," Sangster said, moving his King out of harm's way, "that's where you come in, Ex-Sheriff Burke."

"Ah..."

"You'll convince them that I just took a little vacation," Sangster said, "and that I'm not on the run."

"Well," Burke said, "basically that's true."

"Yes, it is," Sangster said, "so you wouldn't really be lying to the cops."

Burke moved his Knight and said, "Checkmate."

He sat on the ferry with his suitcase between his legs. Inside he had some clothes and about half a dozen disposable cell phones, still sealed in their packages. He wouldn't break the seal on one until he got off the plane in St. Louis.

He hoped that Burke would be able to satisfy the detectives whenever they did come out to Algiers looking for him. Telling them that he had simply taken a trip and would be coming back. He didn't need a state wide alarm to be put out on his "Sangster" name, along with a description. He told Burke he'd call him once, from an untraceable cell phone, and then hold onto the phone for a little while. If the cops did come, and they weren't happy with Burke's story, then the ex-Sheriff would call and warn him. At that point he'd have to take steps to change his appearance—if he had not already done so by then.

The one call he had made from his house before leaving—also on a disposable phone that he tossed away right after—had been to an old contact in St. Louis. It was made only to confirm the contact was still in that City. He'd call again and actually speak to him once he arrived at Lambert International. He had not been to St. Louis in years, but that was where he had to go to find out where Primble was.

The ferry docked, he disembarked and found a cab. If the cops checked they'd find out that he had gone to the airport, just as Burke had told them. And they'd find out at the airport that he'd flown to St. Louis, again just as Burke said. But if they looked further they wouldn't find him. At that point they'd get suspicious. Hopefully, they'd be happy when they found out his destination and wouldn't look any further.

And he could get to work.

SEVENTEEN

It had been at least five years since Sangster had flown into Lambert International airport in St. Louis. He'd been there for one day, fulfilling a contract on an executive at Purina. It was under construction then, and it was under construction now. Most likely *again*, not *still.*

Sangster went immediately to the Enterprise Car Rental counter. He'd used the B.J. Stark false ID to buy his airline ticket. This time he used the one that identified him as Brian Westlake. Before walking to his car, he went into the gift shop and bought a St. Louis Cardinal cap. That and the fact that he hadn't shaved in days was a good enough disguise, for now.

Once he was in the rental car, and before he pulled out of the airport, he broke the seal on one of his disposable phones and dialed a number. When the connection was made nobody spoke.

"It's me."

"Goddamn," a voice said. "I didn't think you'd show."

"I'm just leaving the airport."

"Bourbon, right?" the voice said. "That hasn't changed."

"No," Sangster said, "that hasn't changed."

"Okay," the voice said, "I'll be here with a bottle of Jack."

Sangster broke the connection, started the car and pulled out.

***

It wasn't a long drive to Brooklyn, Illinois, since it was right across the river from St. Louis. It hadn't changed much in five years. Still burnt out buildings among the strip joints—or the other way around. It was right next door to East St. Louis, which still had the highest per capita crime rate in the country.

Sangster pulled into the parking lot of a club called Trickster's, pulled around to the back and parked. He got out and walked to the back door. At this time of the day only the most diehard of deadbeats would be at a strip club.

When the door opened he found himself looking at Mickey Grey.

"Well," Sangster said, "you haven't changed."

"You have," Mickey said. "Nice hat. Come on in."

Mickey Grey was black and had to be about fifty now, but still looked as he did the last time Sangster had seen him five years ago. Now, except for a few grey hairs at his temples, he could still pass for thirty-five.

"What are we calling you these days?" Mickey asked, as he led the way to his office.

"Sangster."

Mickey looked over his shoulder. "Really?"

"Yeah, really."

Mickey shrugged.

They went past a doorway through which Sangster could see two naked girls dancing on two separate stages. They were Mickey's type, big boobs and lots of meat. It was oddly comforting to realize he still didn't believe in hiring skinny girls.

When they reached the office Mickey let him go in first, then followed and closed the door. He then cracked the seal on a bottle of Jack, poured two drinks and handed Sangster one.

"To old friends with new names."

"You're still Mickey."

"I like Mickey," the other man said. He seated himself behind his desk and sipped his drink. For a cheap strip club, the office was impeccably furnished. The wood paneling was expensive, as were the desk and leather chair. Mickey tended to live well behind closed doors.

"So what brings you out of hiding after five years?" Mickey asked.

"I haven't been in hiding."

"No? What do you call it?"

"Retirement."

"Forced retirement?"

"No...not exactly."

"Look, man," Mickey said, "you were at the top of your game. Who quits at the top of their game besides Wayne Gretzky?"

"I did."

"Would it do me any good to ask why?"

"No."

"So you're here to...what? Get back in the game? Why wouldn't you go to Primble for that? Besides the fact that he's a dick."

"I don't know where he is."

"Ah...you're here for information."

"Well," Sangster sad, "five years ago you knew everybody. I assume you still do."

"I know everybody and where they are," Mickey said. "Except you."

"Mickey," Sangster said, "I just need to know where Primble is operating from these days. Is it still L.A.?"

"No."

"I didn't think so," Sangster said. "I mean, I had a feeling..."

"You had a feeling?" Mickey asked. "Have you seen him lately?"

"Yes," Sangster said, "and it didn't go well."

"So...he found you."

"He did," Sangster said.

"I knew he was looking," Mickey said, "but I thought he gave up a long time ago."

"He came to you?"

Mickey spread his arms.

"Am I not the one who knows everyone and where they might be?"

"Except me."

"Which is what I told him."

"Did he believe you?"

"Not at first," Mickey said. "He had this odd idea that you and me were friends."

Sangster didn't comment.

"I told him you didn't have no friends," Mickey went on, "only colleagues."

"And?"

"He finally accepted that." Mickey finished his drink, poured himself another. He held the bottle out to Sangster, who shook his head. "Anyway, I heard he was still looking after that, but figured after a couple of years he'd given up."

"I guess he hadn't."

"Obviously," Mickey said. "Where did he find you?"

Sangster didn't answer.

"Okay," Mickey said, "I assume the reunion was not a happy one?"

"No, it wasn't."

"And now you're the one looking for him."

"Yes."

"To kill him?"

Sangster thought about not answering, but then said, "I don't do that anymore."

"Oh, yeah," Mickey said, "I forgot. You're retired."

"Not just retired," Sangster said.

Mickey waited and when nothing else was forthcoming he said, "You're different."

Sangster hesitated, then said, "Yes."

"I thought so," Mickey said. "As soon as I saw you...it's not in you anymore, is it?"

"No."

Mickey sat back and sipped his drink.

"So what are you gonna do when you find him? How are you gonna handle it?"

"I'm not sure."

"Boy," Mickey said, "you have changed. You used to know exactly what you were doing at all times. Maybe this new you isn't so much better than the old you."

"Maybe not," Sangster said, "but this is the me I'm stuck with now. Do you know where Primble is, Mickey?"

"Yes." Mickey put down his drink, pulled over a pad of paper and wrote down an address. He tore off a piece and held it out to Sangster.

"He's in Vegas."

EIGHTEEN

Sangster had a decent bank balance.

When he decided he had to stop killing it took him a while to decide not to donate the money he'd made over the years to charity. He had to come to terms with the fact that he needed money to live. So he opened an account in a New Orleans bank and from time to time wired money to it from his Swiss account.

So for this reason he was able to return to Lambert from Brooklyn and catch the next flight to Vegas, despite the expense of booking a last minute flight.

When he disembarked at McCarron Airport, he took a moment, sat down in the terminal to decide his next move. Staying in a major hotel wouldn't work. Mickey said Primble had been set up in Vegas for over two years, which meant he had his tentacles throughout the whole city. That was the way he worked. For that reason Sangster had to pick a small motel somewhere outside the city limits.

Then came the question of renting a car. He'd already used the Stark and Westlake names—he'd planned to use the latter to check into the hotel—and didn't want to break out any of the others.

He decided to take a cab. All he had to figure out was where to take it to? This was the time an old-fashioned phone book would come in handy, but he only found a couple of regular pay phone and none of them had books.

Sangster's disposable cell phones were just that, disposable. There was no way to track down a motel. He'd never had a computer, and he didn't have a tablet.

So he was going to have to use on the only other reliable source he knew of.

A cab driver.

At the cab stand he deliberately let the first three cabs go by and went with the fourth. Then driver was black, probably Jamaican, with dreads, in his forties, had probably been driving a cab in Vegas for years.

"Where ya headed, mon?" the man asked as Sangster got in the back with his single bag. "Which resort?"

"No resort," Sangster said, yanking the Cardinal hat down low over his eyes. "Not even a big casino."

"Dat's a switch," the driver said. "What are ya lookin' for?"

"Something small, off the strip, but not too far."

"A motel?"

"Nothing too cheesy."

"Okay, not a motel," the driver said. His license, taped to the back of the front seat, said his name was Huntley. "I t'ink I got the place for you, mon. It's—"

"Don't tell me about it," Sangster said. "Let's go have a look."

"You're the boss." He started the cab and pulled away from the curb.

"Whatcha t'ink, mon?" he asked, twenty minutes later.

"Where are we?"

"Off the Strip, like you said."

"How far?"

"Four miles—might as well be four hundred. I mean,

the Strip's the place to be, and if you're off it, you're off it."

"How far are we from Fremont Street?"

"Even farther than from the Strip."

Sangster looked at the building. It was a smallish casino/hotel called The Boulder. He hadn't been to Vegas in five years, didn't remember this place.

"Is this part of a chain?" he asked.

The driver frowned, turned to look at him. "You don't ask the usual questions most tourists ask, mon."

"Like what?"

"Like which casino has the best buffet? And the best payouts."

"Oh, well," Sangster said, "I'm not really here for those things."

"Then what are you here for?"

"Work."

"What kind of work you do?"

"I'm a writer," Sangster said. "I need to be away from most of the action and noise."

"Well then, mon," Huntley McNabb said, "this is perfect. Best of both worlds. You can gamble when you want, they got a good coffee shop, a small but good buffet and decent rooms."

"It sounds good," Sangster said. "I'll get out here."

"Wait," McNabb said, "I'll pull up in front." He had stopped the cab in front of the building, in the street.

"That's okay," Sangster said, opening the door. "I'll walk. What do I owe you?"

He settled up with the driver and got out.

"Hey, mon," McNabb said, holding something in his hand, "here's my card. Call me if you need a ride."

"Thanks," Sangster said, taking the card, "I will."

The cab pulled away.

* * *

In his room Sangster looked out the window at the street below. He figured Primble would have eyes and ears at all the big resorts, and flophouses. Staying somewhere in the middle should be fairly safe. The same went for using a cab driven by a Jamaican, since Primble hated Jamaicans and never used them in his business. He didn't think they were trustworthy. It had to do with an incident that went back to before Sangster and Primble met. Something Primble could not get past.

Sangster felt pretty secure that he had managed to slip into Vegas undetected—unless Primble had eyes at the airport and he'd been spotted. But he knew of a way to check on that.

His room had a balcony. He slid the door open, stepped outside, and broke the seal on another disposable cell phone.

NINETEEN

Sangster didn't know why people in the business of crime frequented—or owned—strip clubs. That was probably one big part of *The Sopranos* that was true. Mickey owned one in Illinois, and B. Cool owned one in Vegas.

Steven B. Cool—his real name—owned a small club in a low rent section of Industrial Drive, mainly as a dodge to cover up his real business.

Sangster didn't want to keep taking cabs. Sooner or later he'd come across a driver who worked for Primble. And he didn't want to rent a car if he didn't have to. You had to show ID and have a credit card. It had been necessary when he landed in St. Louis, but he didn't want to do it in Vegas.

That meant buying a car—a used one. In fact, a clunker. He needed to find a dealer who sold shit cars. Just four wheels to get around.

But he could use Huntley McNabb for something. So he called him first, while on the balcony, and arranged to meet in front of the hotel in the morning. Then he called Steven B. Cool...

When he came out of the hotel the next morning— once again wearing the baseball cap—the cab driver was waiting out front.

"Hey!" he yelled. "Good mornin', mon. I was glad to get your call." He'd stepped out of the car, was regarding Sangster across the top.

"I need a favor," Sangster said.

"Well, get in and tell me about it."

Sangster got in the back while Huntley slid behind the wheel. He turned and looked at his passenger.

"Where to?"

"I need to buy a car."

"What kind?"

"A shit box," Sangster said.

"Really?"

"I just need it to run for a few days."

"A clunker."

"That's right," Sangster said. "And I want to pay cash."

"Does it have to be a dealer?"

"Why?"

"Well, I know somebody who has a car for sale."

Sangster had planned to ask Huntley to buy the car for him, because he didn't want his name involved. If there was a private citizen who had a car to sell, this would be better.

"Are you worried about papers?" Huntley asked. "A registration? A title?"

"No."

"Then I can get you a good deal, mon."

"I don't care about a good deal," Sangster said.

"Okay, then." Huntley turned around and started the car. "Let's go."

They drove to a house in a rundown neighborhood— the kind of area where the houses had cars and car parts decorating their lawns, back yards and garages. Huntley stopped the cab in front of a one-family ranch that had probably been built in the 60's—and last painted then.

"Who lives here?"

"My cousin. His name is Darnell."

"Okay." Sangster took a wad of cash from his pocket. He'd hit the ATM machine in the casino that morning. The account did not have the name "Sangster" on it, but a DBA name. "Here's five hundred."

"I can probably get it for t'ree," Huntley said.

"If you do that, then you keep the other two."

Huntley smiled broadly and got out of the car. He disappeared into the house. After about fifteen minutes a green Chevy pulled around from behind the house. It idled noisily as Huntley got out from behind the wheel. He walked over to the cab and Sangster got out.

"There ya go, mon," the cab driver said. "It actually ain't bad for a clunker. My cousin, he's a good mechanic."

Sangster circled the car as it continued to idle. The tires were okay, and there was a Las Vegas license plate on the back.

"As long as nobody looks too close at that license plate," Huntley said, "you should be all right. But I wouldn't drive it for more than a few days."

"I don't intend to."

"If you have to, let me know, I can get you a different plate."

Sangster looked at Huntley across the top of the car and said, "Okay. Thanks."

"There's a trunk key," Huntley said, "and a decent spare and jack."

"You did good.'

"Don't you want to know how much it was, mon?"

"I trust you."

"Why?"

Sangster didn't want to tell him it was because he was Jamaican.

"I'm a good judge of character."

"I got my cousin down to two fifty," Huntley admitted.

"That's fine," Sangster said, "You keep the rest."

Huntley smiled broadly, again. "Mon, you need anythin' else, you give me a call, you hear?"

"I hear you, Huntley," Sangster said.

"Can you get back to your hotel?"

"I know the way," Sangster said, but as Huntley pulled away, he got in his new clunker and did not drive back to the hotel.

TWENTY

GLITTER 'N GIRLS was B. Cool's club on International Drive. It may have had a glitzy name and been located in Las Vegas, but as far as Sangster was concerned, it could have been located in Brooklyn, Illinois.

Sangster did the same thing he'd done when he visited Mickey Grey's club. He drove around to the rear and knocked on the back door.

The door opened and a big black dude with a shaved head opened the door.

"Sangster," Sangster said.

"Come on in." The man's voice matched his appearance, a loud bass that rumbled up from deep in his chest. He was wearing a tight T-shirt that showed off all his bodybuilder muscles.

"This way," the man said. "B. Cool is waitin'."

The big bruiser showed him to an office without having to walk past the floor, but from the cars outside Sangster knew that the place was doing well, even at this early hour. After all, time doesn't matter in Vegas.

B. Cool was sitting behind his desk, a cheap blonde wood monstrosity that seemed to take up most of the room. It was chipped and stained and standing on three good legs.

"That's all, Elmore."

"Right." The bruiser left the room.

"Elmore?" Sangster repeated.

"His father liked Elmore Leonard books," B. Cool said.

"*Unknown Man Number Eight-Nine*," Sangster said.

"What?"

"That's my favorite Elmore Leonard novel," he explained. "One of his early crime books."

"Who's got time to read?"

"I do," Sangster said, "these days,"

B. Cool sat back in his chair. Unlike Mickey Grey, he'd aged. He was once a bruiser, like Elmore, but now in his fifties, the muscles had started going to fat. He even had some extra rolls of skin on his bald head.

"Sangster, is it?" B. Cool asked.

"That's right."

"Take off the stupid cap."

Sangster did, holding it in his lap.

B. Cool's pale skin had gone ruddy and he had bloodshot eyes. Never a big drinker when Sangster knew him, that seemed to have also changed. Maybe it had something to do with the fact that he was still doing what he'd been doing ten years ago.

"I was surprised to hear your voice," B. Cool said. "I thought you were dead."

"Not dead," Sangster said, "retired."

"Retired? You ain't even forty."

"Nevertheless..."

"Why the hell did you retire?" B. Cool asked. "Then his eyebrows—or the spaces where his eyebrows used to be—went up. "Wait a minute. Was that why Primble was looking for you? Because you quit?"

"I suppose."

"You were his best man," B. Cool said. "He never would've just...let you quit."

"He didn't let me," Sangster said, "I just did. Mind if I sit?"

"Go ahead."

Sangster sat in one of the two hard, mismatched chairs in front of the desk. It brought him close to B.

Cool, who had the sleeves of his white shirt rolled up and damp patches under his arms even though the office was well air-conditioned. His bald head was dappled with beads of sweat.

"Are you nervous, Cool?"

"No," B. Cool said. "I got high blood pressure and diabetes. I sweat a lot."

"Then why wear long-sleeve shirts?"

"You remember when I had muscles like Elmore?" B. Cool asked.

"I do."

"Well, I don't anymore." That was all he said. Sangster decided he was telling the truth. He wasn't nervous.

B. Cool sat forward, set his forearms on the desk.

"If you're retired," he asked, "what brings you here?"

"Information," Sangster said. "That's still your business, right?"

"Well, it ain't this shithole," B. Cool said. "Whataya need?"

"A few things."

"Shit," B. Cool said. "I'll give you the old friends and family discount."

"Primble lives in Vegas," Sangster said. "I want to know where, and who with. I want to know how many men he keeps around him."

B. Cool frowned. "Primble is your target?"

"I don't have a target, Cool."

"Oh, that's right," B. Cool said. "You're retired. What else?"

"I want to know if Primble knows I'm in town."

"How'd you come in?"

"The airport."

"Take a cab?"

"Yeah," Sangster said, "driven by a Jamaican."

B. Cool smiled. "Ah, retired, but still smart. Where are you stayin'?"

"Off the strip," Sangster said. "Place called The Boulder Casino and Hotel."

"And how'd you get here?"

"Drove," Sangster said. "I bought a car, privately."

"From a Jamaican?"

Sangster nodded.

"Good move. That it?"

"No," Sangster said. "Primble's got two men: Silk Guiliano and Jimmy O'Malley. I want to know everything you know about them."

"And is that it?"

"That's it."

B. Cool sat back and considered the request.

"Well," he finally said, "I can tell you some stuff off the top of my head, but why don't I take the day and look into it?"

"Fine," Sangster said, "take a day."

"Come back tonight," B. Cool said. "I'll fill you in."

"Okay."

"You're gonna need a gun."

Sangster didn't answer. He wasn't sure what to say. He didn't want to kill anyone, but look what had happened in New Orleans? Maybe a gun was a good idea, just to have...

"Don't worry about it," B. Cool said. "I know what you want."

Sangster's needs, when it came to a gun, were always unusual. Nobody in the business could understand it, but Sangster had never trusted the manufacturer of most guns. The last thing someone in his business needed was a gun to misfire or malfunction.

So his wants were very specific.

"I assume nothin's changed there?" B. Cool asked.

"No," Sangster agreed, "nothing's changed."

"Okay then," B. Cool said, slapping both hands on his desk top, "come back tonight, say around one a.m.?"

"I'll be here," Sangster said, standing up and donning the cap. "Thanks, B. Cool."

B. Cool waved his hand and said, "Ah, I ain't so cool no more, Sangster. Them days are gone. I'm just Steve Cool, these days."

"Okay, B. Cool."

They shook hands and B. Cool said, "You can find your way back out, right?"

"No problem."

"And stay off the streets!" B. Cool snapped. "I don't want Primble takin' you off before I can get you armed."

"Don't worry," Sangster said. "I haven't forgotten how to stay alive."

"That's good to hear," B. Cool said. "Damn it's good to see you alive, boy. Now stay that way!"

TWENTY-ONE

Why one a.m.?

Sangster sat in his shit heap of a car in the parking lot behind B. Cool's club, half-an-hour early. Why wouldn't Cool have had him come back in the morning? That's what he was going to find out.

He got out of the car, approached the back of the building. From his pocket he slipped a set of lock picks he hadn't used in some time—but they had been well cared for. Very quickly he worked the locks on the metal door, opened it and stepped inside.

He heard music from the front of house. Back here it was quiet and dark. It hadn't been dark when he was there before, when Elmore let him in. He pocketed the leather case that held his lock picks, but before his eyes could adjust to the interior an arm snaked around his neck from the back.

It was a thick, muscular arm and it immediately cut off his airway. But there was no knee in his back, no torque in the hold. If there had been, he might not have been able to break it. He drove his elbow back, struck a hard slab of an abdomen, did it again and again. Then he stomped on a foot, and the hold was broken. He turned, his eyes having adjusted well enough to see a dark figure. He swung and hit the figure in the face with an elbow that was harder than any fist. The man grunted, and Sangster hit him again. The man slumped to the floor. Sangster followed him down, hit him a third time.

That was it.

The big man was out. Sangster's eyes had now adjusted enough for him to see that it was Elmore. He put his hand on the man's chest, found his breathing measured and stable. His own breathing was under control. He wasn't angry, he hadn't panicked. He had reacted just the way he would have three years or more before.

He left Elmore where he was and walked to B. Cool's office, found the man behind his desk.

"Where's Elmore?" B. Cool asked.

"In the hall."

"Alive?"

"Yeah."

B. Cool nodded.

"Why the test?"

"I just wanted to make sure you could still take care of yourself."

"So you told Elmore to wait for me, grab me from behind and...what?"

"Just...see if you could get away," B. Cool said, spreading his arms.

"He didn't try very hard, B. Cool," Sangster said. "He slipped his arm around my neck, and that was it."

"Well...I told him not to hurt you."

"And now he's unconscious in your hall," Sangster said. "You better have somebody see to him."

"Yeah, right."

Sangster sat down as B. Cool picked up his phone. After a short conversation the man turned back to Sangster and laughed.

"I figured if you were still on your game you'd come early," B. Cool said. "I had Elmore waitin' for you."

"I knew you were up to something," Sangster said.

B. Cool gave Sangster an amused look.

"You didn't think I'd turn on you, did you?"

Sangster shrugged. Who knew how much somebody changed over the years? He knew better than anyone the way a life could change course.

"So how do you think your test went?" Sangster asked.

"I'd probably be more convinced if you had killed Elmore," B. Cool said, "but I guess you haven't completely lost it."

B. Cool got up from his desk, walked over to a cabinet, picked up an attaché case that was leaning next to it. He brought it to the desk and set it down.

"This is what I got for you." He worked the catches and opened the case. Inside were two guns, sitting on a foam bed. Sangster could tell from the indented shapes that the case had not been made to hold the guns that were now in it.

"I remembered those old guns you liked," B. Cool said, "although I could never understand it."

Sangster stared down at the two Webley's. Both were manufactured originally in the 1870's, produced until 1914. Sangster trusted guns produced by Webley, and these two were his favorites.

The larger of the two, the Webley-Fosbery, was a recoil-operated revolver. Once loaded the Webley-Fosbery was cocked by pressing the entire action-cylinder-barrel assembly as far back as it would go. Neither simply pulling the trigger nor manually cocking the hammer rotated the gun's cylinder. Rather, the entire assembly had to be cocked to ensure that a chamber was properly lined up with the barrel.

It came in three barrel lengths: seven and a half, six and four inches. Sangster's choice was always the seven and a half. He found it the most accurate.

For close up work he always preferred the Webley Bulldog. It had a two-and-a-half-inch barrel, fired either .455 caliber or .38 ACP. The .455 came with a six-shot cylinder, while the .38 utilized an eight-shot cylinder. Sangster's choice was the eight-shot. It fired like a normal revolver, just cock and pull the trigger.

Also in the box was extra ammo for each weapon.

But these were his choices from years ago, which B. Cool obviously did remember.

"Okay?" B. Cool asked.

"They're fine." He closed the box. "Do you have the information I asked for?"

"Sure." B. Cool sat back down behind his desk. Sangster sat across from him. The box was a presence between them.

B. Cool opened the middle drawer of his desk and took out some index cards.

"This one has Primble's address on it," he said. "He lives in Green Valley. That's—"

"I know where Green Valley is."

"Okay." He put the card down on Sangster's side of the desk. The ex-assassin did not touch it.

"This one has Silk Guiliano's address on it, this one Jimmy O'Malley's," B. Cool said. "Their neighborhoods are not quite as high class."

"What kind of shape are they in?"

"Well, one of them has a limp, the other one some scars on his face. Other than that they seem...operational."

Sangster leaned forward and picked up the three cards.

"What else you got?"

"O'Malley, he's a gambler," B. Cool said. "Heavy. You'll usually find him at the Riviera—sometimes down on Fremont Street at the Golden Nugget or Binions."

"Sounds like he doesn't like the new Vegas," Sangster said. "Sticks to the old places."

"Lots of real gamblers do," B. Cool said. "You won't find O'Malley playing Texas Hold 'em. He sticks to the old games."

"What about Guiliano?" Sangster said. "What's his pleasure?"

"Well, women," B. Cool said, "except lately he ain't so pretty."

"What kind of women?"

"The kind who would go for a mug like Guiliano," B. Cool said. "Whores, bar bimbos, maybe waitresses."

"No nice girls, huh?"

"Not that I know of."

At that point Elmore staggered into the room. He had a huge welt over his left eye. Behind him came two smaller men.

"Sorry, boss," one of them said. "We couldn't stop him."

"It's okay," B. Cool said, waving them off. "That's all."

The two men nodded and withdrew.

"You look like hell."

"I owe you!" Elmore said, pointing at Sangster.

Sangster stood up and said, "Take it up with your boss."

He faced Elmore, who was between him and the door.

"Stand aside, Elmore," B. Cool said. "Let him go."

The bigger man seethed, the welt on his head seemed to throb, but he stepped aside, reluctantly.

"Another time," he said to Sangster.

"There's no need."

"Yeah," the big man said, "there is."

Sangster started for the door, but B. Cool said, "Hey, Sangster!"

He turned.

"Take the box."

"I won't need it."

"Well, I don't want that old hardware in my place." Sangster hesitated, then walked to the desk and picked up the box.

"What do I owe you?"

"Forget it," B. Cool said. "Old time's sake."

"Thanks, Cool."

"Don't mention it."

Sangster ignored Elmore's hard look, pulled the cap down over his eyes and left the room.

TWENTY-TWO

Eddie Primble sat in his Green Valley home, at his imported Italian marble dining table. His cook—the best private chef he could find in Las Vegas—finished setting the meal out for him, and stood aside.

"Excellent, Martha," he said. "It looks delicious."

"Cooked to your specifications, Mr. Primble," Martha Lyle said. She'd had her own restaurant in Las Vegas until it had suspiciously burned down. Primble was Johnny-on-the-spot with an offer for her to be his private chef. Devastated by the loss, she had accepted the job.

"Thank you, Martha. That'll be all."

"Yes, sir."

Wishing she had put arsenic in some portion of the food, she left the dining room.

He speared a chicken breast from the serving plate, then a healthy portion of vegetables, and then the mixed salad. He was about to dig in when a man entered the dining room, stood by with his hands clasped in front of him, waiting to be invited to speak. Edgar, a gentleman's gentleman, stood tall despite his years—Primble wasn't quite sure how old he was. Seventy? Eighty? A full head of gray hair also made it hard to tell. Jimmy O'Malley called him "Alfred," said he looked like Batman's butler.

"What is it, Edgar?" Primble asked.

"Sorry to interrupt your meal, sir."

"I haven't begun yet, but go ahead."

"It's Silk, sir," Edgar said, "He's at the front door."

"What's he want?"

"I don't know, sir."

"Well, find out."

"Perhaps he wants to have dinner, sir?" Edgar asked.

"That's funny," Primble said. "He still can't chew solid food, thanks to Sangster."

"Yes, sir," Edgar said, "his face is still...uh..."

"Fucked up," Primble said. "All right, show him in."

"Yes, sir."

Primble started to eat. He knew it would bug Silk Guiliano, who still couldn't do much more than drink water—or milk shakes—through a straw.

Edgar came back, leading Guiliano.

"Have a seat, Silk," Primble said. "Edgar, bring Mr. Guiliano a glass of milk and a straw."

Guiliano sat at the other end of the table, a mournful look on his scarred face.

"What's on your mind, Silk?"

It was painful for Silk to speak, so he did so in monosyllables.

"Mon-ey."

"I give you money," Primble said. "You get paid very well."

"Boun-ty," Silk said.

"Oh, the price I put on Sangster?"

Silk nodded.

"You're in no condition to collect that," Primble said. "Neither is Jimmy. And I think we gave Sangster something to think about before we left New Orleans, didn't we?"

"Yeth."

"So then relax," Primble said. "You boys will still get your chance. Believe me, if I know Sangster, he's on his way here—if he's not here already."

Silk looked around, as if he thought the master assassin might come out of the woodwork. Instead,

Edgar appeared, carrying a glass of milk with a straw in it. He set it in front of Silk and withdrew.

"Drink your milk, Silk," Primble said. "Hey, that's funny. 'Milk, Silk.' Get it?"

Silk didn't laugh. He picked up his glass, sipped through the straw, and winced.

"Where's Jimmy, by the way?" Primble asked.

"Ca-sin-o," Silk mumbled.

"Gambling, huh?" Primble said. "No wonder he always needs money."

Silk just shrugged.

"Okay, look," Primble said, "Sangster will be here soon enough. We've got every cab driver and desk clerk on alert, not to mention the cops. When he gets to town, we'll know it."

Silk nodded, put the milk down.

"Now get out so I can eat in peace."

Silk stood up, started to leave. Edgar moved to accompany him.

"Silk!"

He turned and looked at Primble.

"You never told me," Primble said. "Which one of you killed the girl? I know I paid you both, but which one had the satisfaction of wasting her?"

Silk hesitated, opened his mouth to speak, but winced and put his hand over it, instead.

"Okay," Primble said, "never mind. Edgar, show him out."

The two men left and Primble picked up his chicken breast.

Edgar showed Guiliano out the front door, then immediately fetched a can of air spray. He retraced his steps, went everywhere Guiliano had gone, spraying. He wouldn't do the dining room until his master was finished eating.

He sniffed. Pine. Next time he'd try something else. Perhaps peach.

TWENTY-THREE

The apartment building that Jimmy O'Malley lived in wasn't so bad. True, it wasn't in Green Valley, but it was near the strip, not in a ghetto.

Sangster stood across the street, still "disguised." He was waiting for the man to come out, but was surprised when he saw him going in. O'Malley looked like he'd been up all night. Gamblers like him, they did it at night, slept during the day—unless they had a job to do, of course.

He decided not to wait and see what time O'Malley came out. Instead he walked to his shitbox car and drove it to the address B. Cool had given him for Silk Guiliano.

Silk Guiliano's building was more low rent than O'Malley's. Sangster found that surprising, since Guiliano was a better dresser. In fact, Sangster's car didn't look like such a clunker in this neighborhood. In fact, it fit right in.

Guiliano obviously spent his money on clothes, not his digs. And he didn't spend money on his wheels, either. He drove a faded green Dodge Charger.

Sangster picked him up in the morning, coming out of his building. O'Malley was turning in as Guiliano was starting his day. It figured to him that the two men would be that different. It had been reflected in their clothes, and now their lifestyles.

Guiliano wore black pants and a sharp, grey blazer. From across the street and down the block, he couldn't see the man's mouth very well, but knew he couldn't have healed completely by now.

Guiliano walked down the street and got into his Charger. As he pulled away from the curb Sangster followed him. The man drove about two miles and stopped in front of a brick building. He got out and went inside. Sangster parked, got out of his car and walked up to the building. He smiled. It was a medical building, housing several different dentists.

Sangster got back in his car and waited.

He spent the rest of the day following Silk Guiliano. After the dentist, the man drove to a movie theater, a multiplex showing eight different films. He was inside long enough to see two different movies. Luckily, there were a couple of fast food restaurants nearby, which Sangster used for bathroom breaks and take-out, eating in his car.

When Guiliano came out he drove to a small grocery store, came out with two plastic bags, then drove home.

Sangster thought about leaving the man there and going back to his hotel, but he decided to wait. A little after dark Guiliano came out again and got into his car. This time Sangster followed him to a strip club. Then another club. When he went to a third Sangster decided to call it a day.

Back in his hotel room, he wondered what part of Guiliano's day was routine. Certainly not the visit to the dentist. Maybe the movies and the strip clubs? Even the grocery store. The sharp dressed assassin seemed to live a pretty boring life, if this day was any indication.

Sangster decided to spend the next day with O'Malley.

He woke up during the night; his window faced away from the strip. From his vantage point he could see lights, but nothing like the way the strip was lit up, even this late. He could feel it, though. Vegas was always bright and awake.

He turned and walked to the round wooden table on which he had placed the box he'd gotten from B. Cool. He opened it, stared down at the two Webleys. He hadn't touched any guns over the past few years—except the ones Burke would bring over from time to time to show him, and not many of those were able to be fired.

He reached for the Bulldog, pulled back, then finally picked it up. It nestled easily in his hand, warm and comforting. He thought about some of the things Burke had said to him before he left Algiers. If he'd killed Primble, O'Malley and Guiliano, he wouldn't be here and Lily wouldn't be dead. He hadn't killed anyone for money for years, but would it be okay to kill for other reasons? Self-defense? Revenge? Or, now that he acknowledged having a soul, was there any good reason to kill?

Quickly, he put the Bulldog back in the box and closed it. In the morning he was going to have to find somebody who could answer those questions.

TWENTY-FOUR

In the morning, Sangster dug out the card the Jamaican cab driver had given him. He punched the number into one of his disposable phones, realizing that he was going to have to buy a few more.

"'Ello, you have Huntley," a voice said.

"Yeah, this is...you picked me up at the airport"

"I remember you, mon. St. Louis Cardinal fan, right? You didn't want one of the big boys, but you didn't want a dive, either. I got you right?"

"You got me."

"What can I do for you today, mon?"

"You can pick me up at the Boulder," Sangster said.

"When?"

"As soon as you can."

"I'm ten minutes away, mon."

"Good," Sangster said. "Pick me up in the back."

"The back?"

"Yeah, the back parking lot. I'll be there waiting for you." Sangster didn't want to risk any of the valets seeing him. One of them might be working for Primble.

"Okay, mon, I got you. You're the boss. The back parking lot. And where are we goin', today?"

"Today," Sangster said, "we're going to church."

Sangster had decided he needed to speak with a priest. He needed to discuss his dilemma with a man who knew all there was to know about souls. Since he'd only had one for a few years, he hadn't gotten the hang of it yet.

Primble and his boys coming to New Orleans had pushed him to the edge, and he didn't know whether to back away from it or jump off.

He stood in the parking lot behind the Boulder, waiting. His beard had come in real good now, but he was thinking about buying some different caps so he could alternate them. The cab driver had already nicknamed him a Cardinal fan.

True to his word, Huntley arrived in about eleven minutes. He spotted Sangster and pulled to a stop next to him.

"How you doin', mon?" he yelled.

"I'm doing okay," Sangster said, getting in the back.

"Why you call me, mon? Somet'in wrong wit da car?"

"I need to find a church," Sangster said. "I thought you'd know one. It's your town. Where's the nearest church?"

"Dat depends, mon."

"On what?"

"On what kinda Church you want? Catholic, Methodist, Baptist—" Huntley stopped, as if struck by a thought. "Does it even have to be a Christian church, mon?"

Sangster sat silent for a few moments, then said helplessly, "I don't know."

"Well, whatchu need, mon?"

"I need to talk to a priest...or a holy man. Somebody...religious."

"Ah." The black man's face lit up. He turned his head quickly to look at Sangster directly rather than through his mirror, making his dreads dance. "If you trust me, mon, I t'ink I got just the mon for you."

"Well, sure I trust you," Sangster said. "Have you ever steered me wrong?"

Huntley laughed, turned back, put the car in drive and said, laughing, "Not yet, mon. Not bloody yet!"

TWENTY-FIVE

Huntley pulled the cab to a stop in front of a one story house that had seen better days. There was a day when Sangster knew Vegas pretty well, but the town had changed big time since then. First they tried to turn it into a family destination, then realized their mistake and did a reverse. Now he was in a neighborhood he had never seen before.

"What kind of Church is this?" he asked, as Huntley cut the engine.

"Obeah."

"What?"

"Obeah, mon."

"Oh...what?"

"It is a Jamaican t'ing."

"You mean...like Voodoo?"

"No, more like Hoodoo."

Sangster decided not to ask the difference between Voodoo and Hoodoo at that moment.

"It be a religion," Huntley said, "not magic."

"So there's a priest here I can talk to?"

"Not a priest, mon," Huntley said. "Him be an Obeah Mon."

"But—"

"Come on," Huntley said, opening his door. "We will go inside and you will see. Him be a holy man. Dat's what you want, right?"

Sangster supposed. What did he want? Did he think a Catholic priest would hear his confession? Could an Obeah Man do that? But he didn't want to confess. He just wanted some advice or information. Any holy man would do, right?

"Does he know about souls?" Sangster asked.

Huntley had gotten out of the car. Now he stuck his head back in and said, "Him know everythin' about souls, mon."

"Well, okay then."

Sangster got out of the car, followed Huntley up the walkway to the front door. As Huntley reached for the handle of the storm door, Sangster stopped him by putting his hand on the man's arm.

"Is there going to be, like, shrunken heads and things in bottles?"

Huntley smiled, shook his head and said, "Too many movies, my brother."

The cab driver opened the storm door and knocked on. A black man answered. He was tall and lean, like Huntley, but there were no dreads. He was wearing a white T-shirt and jeans.

"Huntley, my man."

"Mahbee."

The two men shook hands, warmly.

"This is my friend..." Huntley said, then realized he didn't know his friend's name.

"Sangster."

"...Sangster," the cab driver said. "He needs to talk to a holy man."

"Come in," Mahbee said.

They entered and Mahbee extended his hand. Sangster removed his hat and shook it. It was dry, with long, slender fingers, firm for a moment, then gone. Then the holy man looked at Huntley and raised his eyebrows.

"I will wait outside."

"Sure," Sangster said.

He looked around the interior of the small house. It was in better shape than the outside. The walls had new paneling, the ceiling looked new, too.

"I do the work myself," Mahbee said. "You want some coffee?"

"Sure."

"Come into the kitchen."

He followed the holy man down a hall to a kitchen that was still being worked on. There were exposed pipes and a floor that had been torn up.

"I'm still working on this room," Mahbee said. "Have a seat."

Sangster sat at a brown wooden kitchen table. Mahbee poured two cups of coffee from a coffee maker on the counter, sat across from him and pushed it over. Sangster was still looking around.

"What were you expecting?" the man asked. "Shrunken heads?"

"Honestly," Sangster said, "I didn't know what to expect. How do you know Huntley?"

"We grew up together."

"He became a cab driver and you became a holy man?"

"Obeah Man," Mahbee said. "My mother was an Obeah Woman."

"And his mother?"

"A maid. Cleaned other people's houses."

"You don't have the same accent he has," Sangster said. "The dreads."

"I don't smoke ganga either." He sipped his coffee. "In some ways I've become Americanized."

"And in others?"

Mahbee grinned. "Still an Obeah Man. What can I do for you, Sangster?"

Sangster hesitated.

"You can talk to me," Mahbee said. "It'll just be between us."

Sangster nodded, sipped his coffee.

"It's about my soul."

"Yes?"

"As far as I know," Sangster said, "I've only had one for about three years."

"Is that so?"

Sangster nodded.

"Go on."

"Before that," Sangster said, "I...did things, for a living. Things I haven't done since."

"Bad things?"

Sangster nodded.

"Okay," Mahbee said, "go on."

"You don't want to know what I did?" Sangster asked.

Mahbee sat back in his chair and said, "I'm going to imagine the worst."

"Good," Sangster said, after a moment, "that's good."

"So what is your question?"

Sangster studied the man for a few moments, then asked, "Are you really a holy man?"

"What do you need to see," Mahbee asked. "An altar?"

"Well..."

Mahbee sighed. "Okay, come with me."

They stood up and Sangster followed him down a hall, past the open door of a bedroom, to a closed door.

Mahbee opened the door and said, "Look."

Sangster stepped forward to peer into the room. The windows were covered. There were candles everywhere, and what looked like an altar. On the walls he saw some jars with...things in them. On the altar was a wooden bowl. The room smelled of incense and...something else.

"There you go," Mahbee said. "An altar. I keep this room as my mother would have kept it."

"Do you use it?"

"When I have to."

"And do we have to today?" Sangster asked.

"Not if we're just going to talk."

Sangster turned, stepped back and looked at Mahbee.

"Are we going to do more than talk?" the holy man asked.

"No."

Mahbee closed the door. "Then let's go back to the kitchen."

TWENTY-SIX

Sangster followed the Obeah Man back to the kitchen, where there was natural light, no candles, no jars and no altar.

"Sit," Mahbee said. "We'll talk." He poured some more coffee. Sangster wondered for a moment what might be in the brew, but he had already had a cup, so that was pointless.

"Tell me about your soul," the Obeah Man said.

"Actually," Sangster said, "I'm here for you to tell me about it."

"What do you want to know?"

"Since I woke up one morning and found that I suddenly had a soul, I've changed my ways. I've done nothing bad."

"But?"

"Some days ago my hand was forced. Someone I know was killed because of me. I need to know if I can exact revenge without losing my soul."

"Revenge?"

"Yes."

"And by revenge you mean that you would have to kill someone?"

"Yes."

"Is that the only way you can get your revenge?"

"I—it may be, but—"

"If you put your mind to it," the Obeah Man asked, "could you think of another way?"

Sangster hesitated, then said, "Maybe."

"Then I suggest you give it some thought."

"But...what if they leave me no way out?"

"Sangster," Mahbee said, leaning forward, "if your heart is true and your soul is true, then whatever you perceive that you must do is true."

Sangster wasn't sure he was hearing right. Was the holy man telling him he could kill and still be true to his soul?

"Wouldn't killing blacken my soul?" he asked. "I mean, that's probably what a priest or a preacher would tell me."

"Then go to them," Mahbee said, "but you should know that Obeah can heal a soul. If you should do what you must do, and you feel that your soul is in danger, come back and see me." The Obeah Man nodded. "We'll go into that room together."

Sangster nodded and said, "Thank you."

They stood up together and shook hands.

"You must decide this, though," Mahbee added, hanging onto Sangster's hand.

"What's that?"

"You must decide if you are a better man with a soul than you were without one," Mahbee said. "Do you really want to keep it?"

Sangster thought a moment.

"You don't have to answer me right now," Mahbee said. "But if you continue on this path, that question will come up again and you will have to answer that question for yourself."

"I understand."

Mahbee walked Sangster to the front door.

Sangster got into the back of the cab. Huntley's head was bouncing to something he was listening to on a pair of earphones. He took them out and turned in his seat.

"Reggae," he said. "How did it go, mon?"

"Fine."

"Did him answer your questions?"

"Yes."

"Him don't look it," the cab driver said, "but him be the real deal."

"I know."

"So you're all set, then," Huntley said, happily. "Where we go from here, mon?"

"Back to my hotel."

"In the back, again?"

"In the back," Sangster said, with a nod.

"You got it, mon," Huntley said, facing front.

As Sangster got out of the cab behind the Boulder Hotel, Huntley said, "You need me again, mon, you got my number."

"I got it," Sangster said, leaning down to peer in the passenger window. He paid Huntley what was on the meter, and then added a generous tip. "Thanks."

"And maybe," Huntley added with a big shit-eating grin, "if you just want to have some Red Stripes and Jamaican honey...you call me?"

"I don't think I'll have time for any of that, but thanks for the offer."

"Well then," Huntley said, "take this. I thought you might need it."

He handed a paper bag to Sangster. He could feel the cold bottles through the paper.

"Thanks."

Sangster waved and walked across the parking lot to the back door.

TWENTY-SEVEN

When Sangster got back to his room, he looked in the bag, pulled out a bottle of Red Stripe. He twisted the cap off and drank it down. Talking about his soul was thirsty work.

He was glad Huntley had given him the six-pack. He stayed away from the bar, and didn't order room service. Bartenders and waiters could also be on the Primble payroll. If he hadn't yet been spotted by any of Primble's eyes, he'd been lucky. He wanted to stay that way.

He opened a second one and sipped it, thinking about what the Obeah Man had told him. If Mahbee was right, at some point he was going to have to decide what he wanted to do about his soul. He was here for revenge, but he had not come prepared to kill. Somehow he had to make sure Primble understood, and never came after him again or sent someone connected to him.

He was going to have to figure out a way.

In the old days, Sangster would have spent time getting to know his target's routine. He'd follow them for days, maybe weeks, until he knew their schedule better than they did. At the same time, in his own life, he made sure he never fell into a routine, so no one would ever be able to do the same thing to him.

But he didn't have the time to do that now.

No, check that.

He didn't have the patience.

Not anymore.

Those days were gone.

He woke the next morning, still thinking about what the Obeah Man had told him. He was going to have to put those questions about his soul aside until the time came. He still didn't have a plan, and that was going to have to come first.

He left the hotel at eight a.m. by the back door, first taking the time to go to the gift shop to buy a Boulder Casino baseball cap. He got into his rattletrap and drove until he spotted a greasy little out of the way diner. The place was a throwback with counter seating. He went inside and grabbed an empty stool. It was easy. There were more empty ones than occupied.

"Help ya?" the waitress asked.

He looked at her. She was staring down at her pad, waiting to write, a strand of brown hair hanging over her eyes didn't seem to bother her. She was pretty, but not in a Vegas way, which was probably why she was working in a diner and not in a casino or hotel as a showgirl or waitress.

"Bacon and eggs," he said. "Coffee, orange juice."

She wrote it all down quickly.

"Comes with home fries. That all right?"

"Fine."

"Toast or muffin?

"English muffin."

She finished writing, tore the slip off her pad and tucked the pen behind her ear. The stray lock of hair was the only piece not pinned up on her head. The name tag on her chest said: LAURIE.

"Comin' up," she said.

"Thank you."

She paused and looked at him for the first time. Maybe she didn't hear those two words very often.

She got him a mug, set it in front of him and filled it with coffee.

"Enjoy," she said.

He picked it up and sipped. It was not very good, but it was strong and hot. He continued to sit as he looked around. There were only a few people in the place, most looked over sixty. Men and women alike, they appeared to be reading the morning paper. No one was paying any attention to him. That was good. He kept his cap on, anyway.

The waitress reappeared, placed a glass of orange juice in front of him.

"Thanks," he said, again.

"Your breakfast will be up in a minute," she said.

"Good." He sipped some juice.

She studied him for a minute, then said, "I haven't seen you in here before."

"That's because I've never been here before."

"From out of town?"

"Yes."

"Why are you eatin' here?"

"You ask most of your customers that?"

She smiled, revealing a slightly crooked incisor on the left side. "Tourists, they usually stay in the big hotels and they eat there."

"I don't like big hotels or fancy restaurants," he said. "I like..."

"Greasy spoons?"

"Exactly."

A bell rang, signaling his order was ready. She went to the window to pick up two plates, set them in front of him. One had greasy bacon, eggs and home fries on it, the other two muffin halves, one overdone and one under. However, they both oozed with butter.

"Okay?" she asked.

"Yes," he said, picking up his fork, "okay."

"Then dig in," the waitress said. "I'll freshen your coffee."

"Thanks."

She cocked her head, grinned and said, "You keep sayin' that."

By the time he had cleaned his plate, she'd refilled his coffee three times. She came over now and said, "Anythin' else?"

"Nope," he said. "That was perfect."

"Perfect?" she asked, smiling. "That's like 'thanks,' a word I don't hear much around here." She set his check down on the counter. "You can pay me."

He looked at the total, took out his wallet and left the money on the counter, with a twenty-five percent tip. He got up and headed for the door. Before he made it she picked up the check and money, saw his tip and said, "Hey, come on back anytime."

He waved as he went out, but doubted he'd ever be back. He intended to find someplace different to eat for each meal, each day.

No routine.

TWENTY-EIGHT

Jimmy O'Malley, the gambler, left his home late in the day. At least, that's what he had done the day before. If he did it again, Sangster would be on his tail. This time, he needed to find someplace to approach him.

Silk Guiliano, on the other hand, left early, so he had probably already missed him.

Sangster drove back to his hotel from the diner. He thought if he was going to face O'Malley he might need the Webley Bulldog. Not to use it, just to show it. But when he got to the parking lot he found Huntley McNabb waiting for him, leaning against the side of his cab.

"What are you doing here?" he asked.

"Waitin' for you, mon. Me don't want to come inside and ask. Me thought, maybe, you don't want to attract any attention." He pointed. "New cap."

"Why would you think that?"

"You have been very careful since you arrived," Huntley said. "You avoided a few cabs before you pick mine, you are staying away from certain hotels..."

"What's your point, Huntley?" Sangster asked, wondering if this guy was going to start being a problem?

"A police detective flew into town today," Huntley said.

"So?" Sangster asked. "How do you know that?"

"Him was showin' his badge and askin' questions at the cab stand."

"And you think this concerns me how?"

"Look, mon," Huntley said, spreading his hands, "I am not tryin' to get into your business. I don't care what you did. To me you just be a good customer. But him was describin', well, you."

"And what did you tell him?"

"Me told him nothin'," Huntley said. "Me play dumb, mon. That is an easy thing for me to do."

"You're not so dumb, Huntley," Sangster said. He looked around the lot, didn't see anyone else. "Tell me what you want."

"Nothin', mon," Huntley insisted. "Me just don't want you to have no trouble."

Sangster studied the cab driver for a few moments, didn't think he detected any guile in the man's eyes.

"What else did he want?"

"He was askin' about you—describin' somebody who sounded like you—but also some other men."

"Who?"

"Me don't know dat, mon."

"Well, what were his descriptions?"

Huntley relayed the information to Sangster, who immediately recognized Silk Guiliano and Jimmy O'Malley.

"What was the detective's name?" Sangster asked. "Where was he from?"

"Ha!" Huntley said, triumphantly. "Me knew you would ask dat." He pulled out a piece of paper, frowned at his own writing. "Him was from New Orleans, and him name was Tel—Tela—"

"Telemaco."

"Dat's him. A big mon, middle-aged—"

"I got it," Sangster said, holding up his hand. "Do you know where he's stayin'?"

Huntley grinned and said, "Me took him there."

* * *

Huntley wanted to drive Sangster to the motel he'd driven Detective Telemaco to, but Sangster thanked him and said no. He did, however, get directions, which he proceeded to follow.

The motel was the kind Sangster had tried to avoid because he thought a poorly paid clerk or maid might be on Primble's payroll. So he pulled up in front, but did not get out of the car. He stayed behind the wheel with his hat pulled over his eyes, arms crossed, sitting low.

Having to check on Telemaco was going to keep him from following Jimmy O'Malley that day. But he had no choice. Certain things needed to be done.

First, he wanted to see the detective to confirm that it was Telemaco.

Second, he had to find out if the man was seriously looking for him, O'Malley and/or Guiliano in connection with Lily's murder.

Annoyed, he sat and watched the motel. He didn't even know if Telemaco was inside. He could already be out pounding the pavement. He didn't feel he had the time to waste just sitting there.

After an hour he pulled out one of his disposable cell phones, realizing again that he was going to have to stop and pick up more.

He dialed B. Cool's number, hoping Elmore wouldn't answer. Instead, it was a girl.

"Who's callin'?"

"Sangster," he said. "Just tell him. He'll take the call."

"Yeah, okay," she said, "chill, dude."

After a moment Cool came on the phone.

"Sangster?"

"I need some help," he said.

"With what?"

Sangster told him.

TWENTY-NINE

When someone knocked on the passenger window within the twenty minute time limit Cool had given him, he jumped, and it annoyed him even more when he saw Elmore peering in at him.

"Just get in!" he snapped. All he needed was for Telemaco to spot a big black guy standing by a parked car.

Elmore opened the door and slid in.

"Whataya need?" he asked.

"There's a man staying at this motel," Sangster said. "I need him watched every minute he's here."

"Who is he?"

"A cop, from New Orleans."

"A cop?" Elmore said. "You want me to follow a cop?"

"And report his movements to me on a cell phone," Sangster said. "I'll give you the number."

"What's he here for?"

"That's what I want to find out."

"You waste somebody in New Orleans?"

"No."

"Was somebody killed in New Orleans?"

"Yes."

"Primble's men do it?"

"One of them," Sangster said. "Probably."

"So he's either here lookin' for them," Elmore said, "or you."

"That'd be my guess," Sangster said. "I can't have him on my ass while I'm doing what I'm doing."

"You still gonna make your hit with a cop in town lookin' for you? Man, who batshit crazy."

"It's not a hit."

"Whatever, man."

"That's why you're going to let me know where he is every hour."

"Every hour?"

"Or more," Sangster said, "depending on how fast he moves around."

Elmore looked at the rundown motel.

"Doesn't look like the NOPD dick got much of a travel budget," he said. "Do we know for damn sure he's in there?"

"Not for sure."

Elmore looked around.

"What if he walks past here and sees you?"

"That's why I want to get out of here," Sangster said, "before he does."

"What if he sees me?"

"Well, he won't recognize you, will he?" Sangster said. "And he's got no authority here."

"What kind of a cat is he?" Elmore asked.

"Middle-aged," Sangster said. "You can take him."

"What's his name?"

"Telemaco," Sangster said, "Detective Telemaco."

Elmore shrugged his big shoulders and said, "You know you can't leave until you point him out to me."

Sangster scowled.

"You're right, damn it." He started the engine. "Let's move."

He pulled further down the street, hopefully to a place where Telemaco would not pass them.

"Where's your car?" he asked.

"Around the corner. Does Telemaco have a car?"

"He didn't rent one at the airport," Sangster said. "He took a cab here. Don't know if he had time to rent one."

"Maybe he'll keep takin' cabs."

"Maybe."

"I could go in and talk to the clerk."

"No," Sangster said. "I don't want to take a chance on the clerk telling him somebody was asking."

"How long are we gonna sit here and wait, then?"

"As long as it takes."

They sat for a few minutes and then Elmore said, "I need some coffee, man."

"Me, too," Sangster said.

"There's a diner around the corner."

"Be quick, then."

The big black man looked at him quickly.

"Why me? I ain't your damn house nigger."

"Do you know what he looks like?"

Elmore firmed his jaw, didn't answer. Sangster doubted the man had ever been anyone's house nigger. He sounded very educated. Probably had some college.

"Okay," Sangster said, "I'll go get it."

"What if he comes out?"

Sangster described Telemaco as best he could, including the clothes Huntley said he'd been wearing when he got off the plane.

"Ah," Elmore said. "I'll go get—"

"No," Sangster said, opening his door, "I need to stretch my legs. I'll be quick. Where's the diner?"

"Around that corner, like I said."

"I'll be right back," Sangster said, slamming the door and walking up the street, away from the motel.

THIRTY

When Sangster walked into the diner he recognized the waitress behind the counter. He hadn't realized that the motel was in the same neighborhood. As he looked around, it seemed as if the same people were still in place, no more, no less. Regulars.

"Back already? New hat, huh?" she asked. "Still hungry?"

"I just need two coffees to go," he said. Every time somebody mentioned his hat he wanted to buy a new one.

"How do you take it?"

He didn't know how Elmore wanted his coffee, so he told her to make one black and one with cream. Whichever one Elmore wanted, he'd drink the other.

She got them together, put them in a drink carrier along with sugars and stirrers. He paid her and turned to leave.

"Have a nice day," she called after him.

He turned and looked at her. She was grinning.

"You, too."

He left, determined not to go back. Twice in one day was way too many times.

"Anybody?" he asked, as he got in the car.

"No," Elmore said. "Did you get me a coffee with milk?"

Sangster handed it over.

"Sugar?"

Sangster passed him a handful of sugar packets and a red stirrer. He took the top off the black and sipped it.

"Just like that?" Elmore asked while he doctored his. "Nothing in it?"

"This is fine."

The black man made a face. He tasted his own, added more sugar.

They sat drinking coffee, and then Sangster handed Elmore his empty container.

"Toss these, will you?" he said. "And pull your car around. But don't put it behind me."

Elmore snorted. "I wouldn't want anyone seein' my ride behind this thing. You couldn't afford anythin' better?"

"This suits me fine," Sangster said. He looked over his shoulder. "Put yours there. You'll be able to get to it quick when he comes out."

"Or goes in," Elmore said, opening his door. "If he's already out."

"Right."

Elmore tossed the containers in a dumpster, then went around the corner for his car. He pulled it up to where Sangster had told him. It was a new Corvette, blue.

"You what?" Elmore demanded.

"I'm taking your car," Sangster said, again.

Elmore pulled the door closed and said, "Oh no, you ain't."

"Well, you can't tail a cop in that thing," Sangster said. "He'll spot you in a second."

"Well," Elmore said, "I didn't know I was gonna be followin' a cop. Cool told me to come here and do whatever you asked me to do."

"Well, I'm asking you to follow the cop in my car," Sangster said.

"What the fuck—" Elmore started, but Sangster cut him off.

"There he is!"

Sangster spotted Telemaco coming out of the motel. He was dressed as Huntley had described.

"Okay," he said to Elmore, "you're on." He put his hand out.

"What?"

"Your keys."

Reluctantly—painfully—Elmore took the keys out and handed them to Sangster.

"Don't scratch it!"

"We'll trade cars again later today," Sangster said. "Make sure you call me." They had already put the number into Elmore's cell phone.

Sangster got out of the car quickly. Elmore slid over behind the wheel, started the engine and took off after Telemaco.

THIRTY-ONE

With Detective Telemaco covered, Sangster could turn his attention back to O'Malley or Guiliano. He could have gone right for Primble but decided to save him for last.

He drove Elmore's Corvette back to his hotel, parked it in the back. It was a lot of car, and he didn't like having it. Sangster was never in love with cars like most men were. To him they were just a way to get from here to there. This one, however, was way too much eye candy for what he had to do.

He went to his room, opened the box with the Webleys in it. He intended to take the Bulldog, but instead just stared at the weapons. It had been a while since he'd fired a gun or even held one with bad intentions.

He checked his watch. If O'Malley held true to what he'd done the day before, Sangster still had a few hours to catch him coming out. If yesterday was not typical, however, he might have missed him already.

Carrying a gun was a risk. If he was stopped by a cop for any reason—an infraction or a perceived infraction—it would mean trouble. With Telemaco in town, the risk was even greater. But going unarmed against a couple of killers was even more of a risk.

On the other hand, he still didn't know if he'd be able to use a gun assuming the occasion presented itself. For show, yes. For effect, maybe. But with deadly force?

He closed the box, took out his phone and dialed.

***

"What happened to your car?" Huntley asked, as he got into the back of the cab.

"I had to loan it to someone."

"Somebody wanted to borrow that car, mon?" the Jamaican asked, with a grin.

"Just drive."

"Where we goin'?"

Sangster gave him O'Malley's address just as his cell phone rang.

"Yeah?"

"I'm checkin' in," Elmore said.

"What happened?"

"Your guy rented a car and drove straight to a police station."

"Are you there now?"

"Yeah," Elmore said, "and I gotta tell ya, I am not very comfortable sittin' outside."

"Are you down the block?"

"Of course," Elmore said. "I'm not gonna sit right in front of damn place."

"Good," Sangster said, "keep me updated."

He broke the connection.

"That the mon you loaned your car to?" Huntley asked.

"Yes."

"Bet him ain't so happy, huh?"

"Hey," Sangster said, "it runs."

"What we be up to today, mon?"

"You're going to drive," Sangster said. "Just drive."

"You be the boss, mon."

Sangster had Huntley park down the block from O'Malley's building.

"What now, mon?"

"Now we wait."

"So," Huntley said, "dis be one of the blood clots you come lookin' for dat we waitin' in?"

"Huntley," Sangster said, "we need to come to an understanding."

"What dat be, mon?"

"You keep the meter running," Sangster said, "and at the end of the night, I'll pay you. But along the way, no questions."

"Dat mean we can't talk?"

"Sure, we can talk," Sangster said, "just no questions."

"Dat suit me, mon," Huntley said. "So, you like Jamaican food?"

THIRTY-TWO

Sangster took several more calls from Elmore before O'Malley finally came out of his building. He'd also been promised by Huntley a breakfast of Ackee and Saltfish and Cornmeal Porridge, and dinner of Brown Stew Fish or Callaloo Stuffed Baked Fish. None of which sounded appetizing to him.

According to Elmore, Telemaco had come out of the police station and then driven to some of Las Vegas' seedier neighborhoods. He then hit the streets.

"I guess the local cops told him where to go to ask his questions."

"How about you find out what some of those questions are, Elmore?" Sangster asked, during the last call.

"Cool told me to do whatever you ask," Elmore said. "Is that what you're askin' me to do?"

"Yeah, it is."

"Okay, then," Elmore said, "but tell me something."

"What's that?"

"What do you have on Cool?"

"That's something you'll have to ask him."

He broke the connection.

When O'Malley finally came out, Sangster said, "Okay, we're on."

"Dat's him?"

"He's got a car, probably down the block," Sangster said. "We're going to tail him."

"You da boss, mon."

"And don't let him see you."

"Me have done dis before," Huntley said. "No worries."

Sangster wished that was true.

They trailed O'Malley to Fremont Street, where Sangster got out of the cab to follow him on foot.

"You want me to come wit' you, mon?" Huntley asked.

"Just stay with your cab, Huntley," Sangster said. "I might need you at a moment's notice."

Disappointed, Huntley settled into the back seat of his cab.

O'Malley hit the Horseshoe, played poker there for a few hours. Sangster had three calls from Elmore during that time.

"He's still hittin' the streets," the black man told him.

"You find out what he's asking yet?"

"Haven't had time, dude," Elmore said. "Once I tail him back to his motel, I'll find out."

That sounded good to Sangster, but he simply broke the connection without commenting.

After a few hours at the Horseshoe, O'Malley's luck must have been bad. He left the casino with a scowl on his face and walked to the Golden Nugget. In the poker room he immediately got a seat at a five-card stud table. They obviously knew him.

In both casinos Sangster was able to sit at a slot machine while he watched O'Malley, slowly playing and hoping he wouldn't hit a jackpot that required a hand payout. He didn't need the attention. For that reason, he chose a nickel machine at the Horseshoe and a penny machine at the Golden Nugget.

O'Malley was easy to tail because he was still walking with a limp from their encounter in Algiers.

Sangster could tell by watching O'Malley's mannerisms that the man was a bad card player. He obviously chased hands and came up empty more often than not.

He had no poker face, whatsoever.

Sangster's cell rang at midnight.

"Yep?"

"He's back in his motel," Elmore said. "I'm hittin' the streets to get you that info you want."

"You sure he's not going out again?"

"No," Elmore said, annoyed, "how in the hell can I know that? But he stopped and got himself some takeout and carried it to his room with him. I think he's gonna eat and turn in."

"Okay," Sangster said. "Talk to you later. Don't call me every hour, just call when you've got something."

"Hey," Elmore started to say, "when do I get my car—" but Sangster broke the connection.

At two a.m. O'Malley quit. He was obviously a loser. As he left the Golden Nugget and hit the street his limp seemed more pronounced because he was walking with anger.

Vegas being Vegas, the street was not deserted, even past two a.m. If Sangster wanted to take O'Malley off the street he would have had to do it with finesse—and without a gun.

He decided to continue tailing him. The man went back to his car, so Sangster had to rouse Huntley from the back seat and get him back behind the wheel.

"Did you win?" Huntley asked, as they pulled away from the curb.

"I wasn't there to gamble and win," Sangster said. "Just stay with him and stay invisible."

"Got you, mon."

O'Malley went directly to his building and went inside. As the door closed behind him Sangster's phone sounded.

"I got what you want," Elmore said.

"Okay, then," Sangster said, "meet me back at my hotel in the rear parking lot."

"How's my car?"

"It's there," Sangster said. "Just park near it and I'll meet you there."

This time it was Elmore who broke the connection.

"Back to the hotel?" Huntley asked.

"Yeah, but park on the side," Sangster said. "I'll walk to the parking lot."

He didn't want Huntley to see Elmore and vice versa.

THIRTY-THREE

Huntley dropped Sangster off around the corner. After receiving a generous tip, the cab driver told him to call if he needed anything else.

When Sangster reached the parking lot, he saw that he had beat Elmore there. In minutes he saw his rattletrap car pull in. Elmore obviously spotted his Corvette, parked Sangster's car a few spots away from it. Sangster intercepted him as he got out.

"Here." He tossed the man his keys. Elmore caught them one handed, returned the favor.

"Now what?" the big black man asked.

"Just stay right here and talk to me."

"I want to check my car."

"Later."

Two men standing next to Sangster's shitbox would attract no attention. However, two men standing next to a new blue Corvette, especially one black and one white.

"What have you got for me?"

"You're in the clear."

"Why do you say that?"

"That detective spent the day looking for anybody who knew a man named Stark."

Sangster kept it to himself that he was not at all in the clear.

"Anything else?"

"He had a couple of descriptions of two other men, but no names," Elmore said. "Sounded like Primble's boys, though. O'Malley and Guiliano. Who's the Stark guy?"

"Never mind."

"Oh, wait," Elmore said, "that's you, isn't it?"

Sangster didn't answer.

"Did Telemaco leave his phone number with anyone?" he asked.

"He left it with everybody," Elmore said. "Odd area code, so it must be his cell."

Sangster took a minute to think. He needed more information on what Telemaco was doing in town, and he could only think of one way to get it.

"Elmore, I need you to call him."

"Call...who? The cop?"

"Right."

"What the hell for?"

"I want you to give him B. Cool's name."

"What the fuck—"

"I need to find out what he knows," Sangster said. "If you call him, tip him that B. Cool is the man in town who knows everybody, then Cool may be able to find out for me."

"We can have somebody call him and pretend to be—"

"No," Sangster said, "before he agrees to meet anybody he'll check them out with the locals. Cool will check out."

"I can't do that on your say so, Sangster," Elmore said. "I'll have to check with B. If he gives the okay, then I'll do it."

"Suits me," Sangster said.

"Okay I check my car now?"

"Yeah," Sangster said, "I'll call Cool tomorrow. You can tell him."

"I will," Elmore said. "Get a new hat, will you? That's lame."

"Like what kind?"

"Try UNLV," Elmore suggested. "Or just one that says Las Vegas."

"Thanks for the tip."

"My car ain't scratched?"

"I didn't even use it," Sangster told him. "I drove it here and took a cab."

"You left it alone in this parking lot?" Panicked, Elmore ran to his car.

THIRTY-FOUR

Sangster started the next day by doing some shopping.

He had breakfast in a nearby McDonald's, grabbing it in the drive-thru and eating in his car. Then he drove around until he spotted an electronics store where he bought six disposable cell phones.

"Lots of people do business this way now," the clerk said, as he rang him up.

Sangster did not reply, but that didn't stop the clerk from continuing.

"Hardly anybody's got a landline in their house anymore."

Sangster nodded, abruptly grabbed two hats from a nearby rack.

"These, too."

One had UNLV on it, the other said LAS VEGAS ROCKS.

"Yes, sir," the clerk said. "The 'Las Vegas Rocks' is very popular."

Again, Sangster nodded. He paid cash for his purchases and went back to his car. He dumped five of the phones in the back seat with the hats, broke the seal on the sixth and proceeded to dial B. Cool's number. He had to go through another girl before getting the man on the line.

"Elmore tell you what I wanted?"

"He did," Cool said.

"And?"

"I don't like talkin' to cops," Cool said, "but this guy's from New Orleans. How bad could a hick cop be?"

"A cop's a cop." Sangster said. "Don't underestimate him."

"I told Elmore to go ahead and make the call," Cool said, ignoring the advice. "I'll let you know when I hear from him."

"Use this number," Sangster said. "It'll be good all day."

"Right."

"Thanks, Cool."

"I still owe you, man," Cool said.

"After this trip," Sangster said, "we'll be even."

"Yeah, well, we'll see."

Sangster broke the connection, pocketed the cell phone. He started the engine and drove to Silk Guiliano's building.

He parked down the block from Guiliano's building, grabbed the LAS VEGAS RULES cap from the back seat and jammed it onto his head. This would be the second time he tailed Guiliano. But after this he was going to have to make some decision about what to do now. He had no more time or patience to figure out patterns, and even less of each now that Telemaco was in town.

He checked his watch. It was almost 9:40 a.m. He expected Guiliano to come out any minute, but instead got an unpleasant surprise.

A car pulled up in front of the building and a man got out.

It was Detective Telemaco.

Sangster stared, narrowing his eyes. Yeah, it was him, all right. How the hell had he found out where Guiliano lived?

He watched as the detective went into the building. If Primble's man had killed Lily and Telemaco arrested him, that would not satisfy Sangster. He needed to make it clear to Primble that he should never approach him again. Telemaco was getting in the way of that.

There was nothing he could do at the moment, though. Telemaco was in town looking for Primble's men. He either didn't have their names or didn't want to use them. Either way, he was describing them. And he may have thrown the Stark name around just for the hell of it. Sangster certainly didn't want to run into the man. He had no choice but to remain in the car and watch.

Waiting and watching turned out to be the right thing to do.

There was an alley running alongside Guiliano's building. No sooner had the detective gone inside then the hired gun came skulking out of the alley. He looked both ways, then ran down the block toward his car, keeping an eye over his shoulder as he went.

Somehow, Telemaco had found Guiliano.

Somehow, Silk Guiliano had seen him coming.

Sangster started the engine of his car, and when Guiliano pulled away from the curb, he followed. He watched his rear view mirror, but there was no sign of Telemaco.

This probably suited him just as much as it suited Silk Guiliano.

THIRTY-FIVE

Guiliano drove directly to the Green Valley area of Las Vegas. Sangster knew this was where the money lived. That meant Primble was there. He had meant to concentrate on the two hitters—O'Malley and Guiliano—first, and had not even asked B. Cool yet for Primble's address. This was a bonus for him.

They drove past the Green Valley Ranch Resort, proceeded for another mile or so until Guiliano came to a stop in front of a gate. It was close enough for Primble to say that Green Valley was his neighbor.

The walls on either side of the gate were about eight feet tall. Guiliano leaned out his window, pressed a button and spoke. He withdrew his head, the gates opened, and he drove in.

Sangster wanted to drive up to the gate, but didn't know if there was a security camera hooked up. He parked a hundred yards away and made his way on foot. He carefully looked over the area in front of the gate. He saw the intercom system Guiliano had spoken into, but nothing to indicate that it was combined with a camera.

He kept his back against the wall and proceeded to give the matter some thought.

Silk Guiliano stopped his car in front of the great house and got out. He gazed up at the structure, as he always did. It had been built twenty years before by a gambler with money he'd won over a weekend at the Golden Nugget. As the story went, three days after he finally moved in, he died of a heart attack. He was eighty-three at the time.

Since then it had been owned by a Vegas performer, a politician and a playboy. Primble had bought it just two years ago.

He walked to the front door and rang the bell. The door was opened by that creepy Edgar.

"Mr. Guiliano," Edgar said. "Follow me, please."

Guiliano followed Edgar from the entry foyer into a hall. He hoped that Primble wasn't eating this time. Thankfully, he wasn't. Edgar led him to the opulent living room, where Primble was standing among the overstuffed furniture and varied pieces of what he called art. Guiliano didn't know anything about art, but he thought his boss's taste was horrible.

"Silk."

"Boss."

Primble was wearing a purple smoking jacket. He had them in half a dozen different colors, all equally painful to look at.

"What brings you here in such an all-fired hurry?"

"A cop."

"What cop?" Primble said. "We don't have anything to fear from the cops."

"Not a local cop," Guiliano told him, "a New Orleans cop. A detective."

Primble frowned. "What's an NOPD detective doing here?"

"Askin' questions," Guiliano said, "questions that led him to my building."

Primble frowned. This was not good news.

"Where has he been asking these questions?"

"The streets."

"Is he asking for you by name?"

"No," Guiliano said, "He's describing me and O'Malley."

"Both of you?"

"Yeah."

"Do we know why? Exactly?"

"No," Guiliano said, "but we can guess."

"The woman."

The assassin nodded.

"What else was he asking?" Primble asked.

"He did mention a name," Guiliano said. "Stark."

"Who is Stark?"

"I don't know."

Maybe that's who the cop was really after.

"Did he see you?"

"No," Guiliano said, "I went out the side door as he came in the front."

"This is not good," Primble said. "We've been expecting Sangster, not a cop. Do you have his name?"

"Telemaco," Guiliano said, "Detective Telemaco."

"How did you find that out?"

"I have eyes and ears on the street."

Primble knew Guiliano would not give up his source, so he didn't ask.

"So what do we do?" Guiliano asked. "Do you want me and O'Malley to kill him?"

"Killing a cop—even a New Orleans cop—would cause more harm than good."

"Then what?"

"I'll have to think about it," Primble said. "Meanwhile, don't go home. Do you have someplace safe to stay?"

"Yeah, I do."

"And O'Malley," Primble said. "Tell him to make himself scarce."

"It'll be hard to keep him from the casinos and card rooms," Guiliano said. "Usually, you have to take him out of town or give him a job."

"Okay," Primble said, "then tell him his job is to stay scarce."

"I'll try," Guiliano said, "but that crazy fuckin' Mick is stuck on gambling. The only thing he likes better is...killing."

"All right. Then tell him he'll get to kill somebody," Primble said. "Just don't say who or when."

"What are you gonna do about the cop?" Guiliano asked.

"Don't forget," Primble said, "I have eyes and ears of my own." More than you, Primble thought. "Show him out, Edgar."

"This way, Mr. Guiliano."

"Stay in touch, Silk."

"Sure, Boss."

He turned and followed Edgar to the front door.

THIRTY-SIX

Sangster was still standing with his back against the wall when the gates swung open. He dropped to his knee, tried to make himself smaller. Guiliano's car came out, turned away from him and instead of going back the way he had come, went in the opposite direction.

Sangster didn't have to wonder what the meeting was about. Guiliano had run right to his boss to tell him about Detective Telemaco.

The gates were closing slowly. If he moved quickly he could get inside the walls. Hopefully no one was watching the camera. Maybe he'd go unnoticed, for a while anyway.

He decided to risk it.

Edgar came back into the living room.

"He's gone, sir."

"Okay, Edgar," Primble said. "Tell cook I'll have tea now."

"Yes, sir. I'll go and...spray first."

He wanted to use his new Peach can. Maybe someday he'd find the right scent to mask Guiliano's odious cologne.

Primble stared at the Klee painting on the wall. It was his newest purchase, but staring at it now gave him no pleasure.

He thought about the name Guiliano said the detective was asking about. Stark. That had to be an alias Sangster was using, maybe whenever he was with the woman. If Telemaco only had descriptions of Guiliano and O'Malley, then maybe he'd forget about them if he had a lead on Stark.

Primble did have eyes and ears in Las Vegas—many of them. He still hadn't heard a word about Sangster being in Vegas...yet. But he must have arrived by now. The Sangster he knew wouldn't have the patience to put it off.

Could it be that Sangster had actually lost it? Was that why he hadn't killed any of them in New Orleans? He'd been brutal in his attacks on Guiliano and O'Malley, but he hadn't been able to kill them.

Was Primble wrong? Was Sangster not coming for him, after all?

But if the detective was here, and "Stark" was, indeed, Sangster, then his ex-agent of death was no longer in New Orleans. And if he wasn't in Las Vegas, then where was he?

Where?

THIRTY-SEVEN

Sangster was inside the walls.

If there was a camera on the front door, there had to be cameras throughout the grounds. There was also foliage—a lot of it, overgrown, but well cared for. He kept to the bushes as he moved nearer the house.

Abruptly, he wished he had the Bulldog with him.

But if he got to Primble now and killed him, would it be over? No, because Primble didn't kill Lily, one of his hitters did. Sangster's revenge had to be taken on all three of them.

His revenge.

Revenge without murder.

He crouched behind a shrub nearest the house, waiting. If anyone had seen him they'd probably be coming after him.

After ten minutes there was no alarm and no security. Thankfully, no dogs.

He broke for the house. On a terrace along the side of the building, which was huge, he shook his head. Primble must have been doing very well for himself to live in a place like this. Profiting off the death of others for as long as he had...something Sangster had helped him with for a very long time.

Sangster felt a moment of shame.

He examined the windows and French doors on that side of the building very carefully. They were all wired. Sangster's past experience was as an assassin, not a burglar.

He couldn't get in without setting off an alarm.

Sangster was surprised at the absence of armed guards. Primble must have felt pretty secure inside the mansion. If Sangster had wanted to get inside, he would need the assistance of someone else, someone who could bypass an alarm system. To find such a person he'd have to use B. Cool again. Only this time, he might have to pay.

But Primble was third on his list. Silk Guiliano and Jimmy O'Malley were first and second.

What he had to do now was get off of Primble's property the way he had gotten on it—without being seen.

Edgar came into the living room and regarded Primble, who was seated on the sofa, holding his tea cup.

"Sir?"

Primble turned his head and stared at Edgar. He didn't act it, but the servant knew he'd startled his master.

"Excuse me," he said, "but I thought I'd clear away the remnants of your tea before checking the camera feeds."

"Of course," Primble said. He leaned forward, put the tea cup down on the tray resting on the coffee table on front of him. "Remove it."

Edgar nodded, moved forward and picked up the entire tray.

"Is there anything else I can do?" he asked.

"No," Primble said, "I'm processing everything that's happened. I'll come to a decision soon. Just keep me informed about the camera feeds."

"Yes, sir."

Edgar left with the tray.

Primble sat back, returned to where his thoughts were before he was interrupted.

He couldn't quite believe it, but he was thinking about killing a cop. They didn't need this Telemaco nosing around when Sangster finally put in an appearance. Primble either had to figure out a way to get him to leave—or get rid of him for good.

Edgar entered the security room. He was paid by Primble to multi-task. He performed the functions of a butler and head of security. His employer's greatest fault was that he was cheap. Or the simple fact that he was cheap. Rather than hire a security staff that he'd have to pay each week, he made a one-time purchase of a security system and hired Edgar to maintain it. Even when Edgar requested a staff of simply two men he was turned down.

He sat in front of the monitor and began to scroll back through the past couple of hours. There were cameras installed throughout the estate, segregated into quadrants. He examined the feeds, looking for anything out of the ordinary. These feeds should have been watched live, but he could never convince Primble of that. The man thought he was invincible behind his eight foot walls. And even if anyone did make it onto the grounds, he was sure they could not breach the security of the house.

He was wrong, of course, but Edgar could not convince him of that. Primble's ego would never allow it.

But the man paid Edgar well, so he continued to perform his various duties as well as he could.

He played back the feeds from each camera, checking each quadrant. Up to now no one had ever breached the walls, but as he watched he saw someone do it with relative ease. He leaned forward, watched the man slip through the gates before they closed behind the departing Silk Guiliano.

He shook his head mournfully. It was just as he had always feared. He had no choice but to report the break-in to Primble.

"Can you zoom in on him?" Primble asked, moments later as Edgar played the tape back for him.

"Of course."

The touch of a few keys and the camera zoomed in on the man's face.

"Is it him?" Edgar asked.

"Yes," Primble said, "yes, goddamnit, it's him. It's Sangster."

Edgar remained silent.

"Don't say it," Primble said. "What's the time stamp on that?"

"About fifteen minutes ago."

"Call for some men," Primble said. "If he's still on the grounds, I want him found."

THIRTY-EIGHT

Fifteen minutes later Sangster realized why there were no guards or dogs. The eight foot walls were not scalable. While there was a lot of foliage on the grounds, three trees had been cut back from the walls so they couldn't be used. Someone would have to come equipped with climbing gear.

But, on the other hand, he'd been able to waltz right through the front gate. Was that the kind of glaring oversight Primble could live with? Probably. The man had a huge ego, even if his fly was open he'd never want anyone to point it out. Least of all an employee.

While no one had yet come out of the house looking for him, he couldn't count on that situation going on much longer. Even if no one was viewing the cameras live, someone was bound to study the tapes eventually. At the very least they would, at some point, see him coming through the front gate.

He wondered if he'd be able to get out the same way he got in, through the front gate?

"How long?" Primble asked Edgar.

"Ten minutes, tops."

"Okay," Primble said, "you get out there now. Go to the front gate and wait for him?"

Edgar walked to a cabinet against the wall, opened it and took out an AK-47.

"I can take care of him."

"Don't be an ass," Primble said. "Sangster's the best I ever saw. If he has a gun, you'll be dead."

"Didn't you say he's been out of it for years?"

"The man's a natural killer, Edgar," Primble said. "He's forgotten more about it than you ever knew. Just do as I tell you."

"Yes, sir."

"Of course—"

Edgar had started for the door, but Primble's voice arrested the movement.

"Yes?"

"If you happen to see him," Primble said, "and you have a shot..."

"Yes, sir."

Edgar went out.

Primble sat down to watch the live camera feed.

As Sangster approached the front gate, three SUV's came to a stop just outside. This was the security presence he'd been waiting for.

He took cover in some foliage just in time to miss being seen by an older man carrying an AK-47. The man swung open a small metal box set in the wall and pulled a switch. The gate started to open.

He and the security men stood together a moment and talked. Actually, he did all the talking and they listened. Then they all piled back into their SUV's, drove through the gate and up the drive as the gates closed behind them.

The man with the AK-47 looked around, then started walking up the drive in their wake.

Primble watched on the camera as Edgar spoke with the security men, then continued to watch as the SUV's drove through the gate. Edgar stood in front of the gate as it closed, looking around, then walked out of the frame.

Primble continued to watch, even as he heard the SUV's pull up in front of the house. Edgar would handle them. He kept his eyes on the screen.

Sangster studied the gate. The walls may not have been climbable, but the gate looked to be. It was quite ornate, and the design between the bars of the gate could be used as footholds.

If he was going to do it, he'd have to do it fast. If security was there, somebody was bound to be watching the live camera feed.

Maybe even Primble, himself.

As Primble watched, Sangster came into view. He grabbed the gate, as if testing its strength. Primble thought maybe he should have gone for the extra money to electrify it.

Sangster put one foot up, preparing to climb over. Then he stopped, turned and looked back. He didn't know exactly where the camera was, but he smiled and waggled his finger at Primble, whose face suffused with blood.

Sangster then put a foot up on the gate, then stiffened and stepped away. Primble switched over to the camera outside the gate and saw the reason why.

THIRTY-NINE

Sangster saw the two police cars pull up in front of the gate, along with another car he recognized. It was the rental Detective Telemaco was driving.

As the men got out of the car, he saw two uniforms and two detectives who looked like doubles for Telemaco and his own partner—one younger, one older.

He stiffened, backed away from the gate and then took cover in the bushes.

Telemaco joined the Las Vegas detectives in front of the gate.

"This fella Primble lives here?" he asked.

"This is it," Detective John Crichton said.

"He bought it with blood money," his partner, Detective Dudgeon said.

"Why haven't you put him away?"

"You must have some bad guys where you come from who you just can't get enough evidence on," Crichton said.

"Oh, yes," Telemaco said.

"Well, there you go," Dudgeon said. "Primble's never pulled a trigger himself."

"I see," Telemaco said. "Yes, we have our own problems like that, men who use others to do the dirty work. Can we get inside to talk to him?"

"Oh, yeah," Crichton said. "We've been inside a few times. He's always very polite and cooperative."

"Well," Telemaco said, "let's see how polite and cooperative he'll be with me."

Crichton nodded and pressed the buzzer.

Edgar entered the security room.

"Sir?"

"The cops are here, damn it," Primble said. "Where are our men?"

"Searching the grounds."

"All right," Primble said, standing up. "Let me get to my den and then let them in."

"Sir?"

"They want to talk to me," Primble said, "and I want to see what they want."

"But what about Sangster?"

"Tell the men to keep searching for him."

"Yes, sir."

"And you...just be you. Understand?"

"Yes, sir."

The outside buzzer sounded again. This time Edgar answered it.

"May I help you?"

The door opened and Telemaco saw a tall, thin man of indeterminate age in the doorway.

"Detective Telemaco," Crichton said, "meet Edgar. He's is Primble's major domo."

"Edgar," Dudgeon said, "we're here to talk to your boss."

"Of course," Edgar said, "but who exactly is this gentleman?"

Telemaco took out his badge.

"New Orleans?"

"We're offering our friend from Louisiana a helping hand," Crichton said. "He's investigating a murder, and his search has brought him to Las Vegas."

"How distressing."

"I assume Mr. Primble is in?" Crichton said.

"Of course," Edgar said, "but perhaps they can wait outside?" He was referring to the two uniformed officers standing behind the detectives.

"Sure," Crichton said. "You boys wait right here."

"Yessir," one of them said.

"Follow me, please," Edgar said.

The three detectives followed Edgar, single file, until they reached a doorway.

"Sir," Edgar said to someone in the room, "the police are here to see you."

"Well, bring them in, Edgar," Primble said. "Don't keep our friends waiting."

"Gentlemen," Edgar said, stepping aside to let the police detectives enter the room.

Sangster remained in hiding while the detectives drove in and up the driveway. He considered going back up to the house, hoping to see or hear anything, but there were two good reasons not to do that.

One, he'd made a mistake by coming onto the grounds in the first place. The risk had been too great and he had learned nothing.

Two, there were now a cadre of security men looking for him on the grounds.

He could have remained in hiding until the detectives drove out, and slipped off the grounds the same way he got on, through the closing gates. But if he did that he was taking a chance he'd be discovered before he had a chance to leave.

Thankfully, he heard no dogs.

He decided to stick to his original plan. Scale the fence and get out of there.

He broke from his cover, ran to the gate and quickly climbed over. Any lack of conditioning he suffered from three years of inactivity had been counteracted by adrenaline.

FORTY

"You were in New Orleans," Telemaco said.

"Yes, I was," Primble said. "I stayed at the Lafitte House and quite enjoyed myself. You have a lovely city."

"But you never heard of a man named Stark?"

"I'm afraid not."

"And you didn't have two men with you?"

"I've told you," Primble said, "I don't know what two men you're referring to."

"Two men were seen around your hotel," Telemaco said, "then they were seen on the Algiers ferry with a third man. The descriptions of the two men are the same."

"And the third?"

Telemaco colored a bit.

"I don't have a good description of him."

"Well," Primble said, "I'm afraid I never got a chance to see anything other than the French Quarter. This other area..."

"Algiers Point."

"...yes, and a ferry? I'm afraid I would not have done well on a ferry. I don't like the water. Could I have gone to that area by car?"

"Yes," Telemaco said, "there's a bridge."

"Well, next time I'm in your fair city," Primble said, "perhaps I'll do that."

He looked at the two Las Vegas cops. They had been quiet throughout Telemaco's interview.

"Is there anything else I can do for you gents?" he asked.

Instead of answering, the two men looked over at Telemaco.

"No," the New Orleans detective said, "I guess that's it. Thanks for your cooperation."

"Edgar will see you out, then," Primble said.

Sangster got into his car and drove away before any of the security men could spot him and come after him. For a moment he thought the car might not start, but then it turned over.

He drove toward his hotel, steering through the first fast food restaurant he came to—a Wendy's—on the way.

He entered his room with his bag of food, sat on the sofa, spread the food over the coffee table and started to eat. He was angry with himself and he was trying to suppress it with a hamburger and fries. He washed down a mouthful with a sip of Coke, then wiped his mouth and sat back.

His first mistake was even entering the property when he wasn't prepared. In the old days he never would have acted that impulsively. Second, waving at Primble through the camera. That was childish, foolish, and it left no doubt in Primble's mind but that he was in Vegas. Now it would be harder for him to move around the city because Primble would have people actively looking for him rather than just being on the lookout.

He might have gotten away without being recognized because of the hat and the beard, if he had not gotten cute and waved.

He popped a French fry in his mouth and chewed thoughtfully. Had he wasted his time coming here? Was he simply unable to fulfill his promise to himself to make them pay for killing Lily for no reason? He didn't even know her that well. Nevertheless, he felt responsible for her death, and there was a lot of guilt connected to that.

Guilt.

Was that the price he paid for having a soul? When he awakened that first day—the first day he had a soul—he'd been overcome with not only guilt for all the people he had killed, but grief. It had taken him a long time to get over it—well, to get over it enough to become mobile again. To start living—perhaps for the first time in his life.

Even as a child Sangster had not known the meaning of guilt or grief or joy or any of the emotions other kids around him seemed to revel in.

He had never been arrested. His fingerprints were not on file anywhere. If he had even been caught and jailed, and a court appointed psychiatrist examined him, he was sure he knew what name they would have labeled him with.

Sociopath.

But that was the man he used to be, not the man he was now.

He bit into his burger and chewed listlessly. He'd eat the food because his stomach was growling, but he couldn't taste it.

When he finished eating he put all the empty containers in the bag, dropped it in a nearby trash basket. He was still angry—or maybe he was disappointed, in himself.

He went into the bathroom, washed his hands and face, dried them and then stared at himself in the mirror. He was still wearing a UNLV hat. Primble—or somebody—had seen the hat on camera. He'd have to throw it out, wear one of the others or get some new ones.

He went back into the other room, sat on the sofa. He'd taken one of his cell phones from the back seat. Now he broke the seal and dialed B. Cool's number. There was no answer. It rang ten, twelve, fifteen times, and no answer.

That wasn't good.

Not good, at all.

Without talking to B. Cool he didn't know where Elmore was.

He grabbed the other cell phone—the one Elmore had called him on. The black man's number was stored there. He brought it up and dialed. It, too, rang and rang without answer.

Something was up.

He checked his watch. By now Primble would have warned both Guiliano and O'Malley about him. Following them was not an option anymore.

He picked up the remote, and pointed it at the TV.

Primble sat behind his desk, fuming and waiting.

Edgar walked in, and he looked up.

"Anything?"

"No, sir," Edgar said. "Apparently, he didn't get into the house."

"The men?"

"I sent them away."

"And the police?"

"Gone."

"Edgar," Primble said, "I want to know why those detectives brought that New Orleans detective here to see me."

"Sir?"

"Somebody put him on to me. And I need Guiliano and O'Malley."

"I've sent for them."

"Good."

"Sir?"

"Yes?"

"Are you quite sure it was him?" Edgar asked. "I mean, the hat, the beard—"

"It was him," Primble said. "He wanted me to know it was him."

"Then...if he's so good, why didn't he get in?"

"Maybe," Primble said, "he didn't want to."

Edgar raised his eyebrows, as if he hadn't thought of that.

FORTY-ONE

The TV was on, but Sangster wasn't looking at it. Instead, he was looking at the box that held the two Webleys. He had made some mistakes since coming to Las Vegas. He didn't want to make any more. With Telemaco in town and Primble now aware that Sangster was here, things had changed. Only the fact that he had not registered at the hotel under the name Stark was keeping them from finding him.

His next decision might be the most important of his life.

Primble looked up as Edgar entered the office.

"Have you got something for me?"

"Yes, sir," Edgar said. "We know who gave the New Orleans detective your name."

"Was it one of the Vegas detectives?"

"No, sir," Edgar sad. "It was B. Cool."

Primble sat back in his chair.

"That actually figures," he said.

"What shall we do?"

"I've co-existed with that man in this town long enough," Primble said. "Give the order to Silk and O'Malley."

"Sir? Is that wise? With the police—"

"Do it, Edgar," Primble said. "Any word on Sangster?"

"No, sir," Edgar said. "We have not located him yet."

"All right," Primble said. "Keep our people looking."

"Yessir."

"Oh, and Edgar."

"Yes?"

"Have that front fence electrified."

"Yessir."

"And I want someone on those cameras twenty-four hours."

Edgar nodded and left.

Primble was plugging the holes, closing the barn door after the horse was gone, but he had to make sure this didn't happen again. His own arrogance had allowed Sangster to breach his walls. And his own arrogance had caused him to leave Sangster alive in New Orleans. Even after Sangster had disabled both O'Malley and Guiliano, he could have brought in more men. Instead, he'd made sure Sangster would come to Vegas. It may have been a mistake, but now he had to deal with it.

Or have it dealt with.

Hours later Sangster was still sitting in his hotel room. Indecision had him paralyzed. It was not a feeling he'd ever had to deal with before. Even after he decided to give up being a paid assassin, he was able to make his decisions with authority.

Abruptly, his disposable cell rang. He frowned. Who had the number? He only used the phones to make calls, not receive them. Then he remembered Huntley.

"Huntley, that you?" he asked.

"No," a voice said, "it's Elmore."

"Hey, where've you been?" Sangster asked. "I've been trying to call you or B. Cool."

"B. Cool's dead."

"What?" Sangster asked. "When did that happen? Where?"

"A little while ago," Elmore said. "They came into the club, took me out from behind. I never knew what hit me. When I woke up, B. Cool was in his office, dead. They cut out his tongue and left it on the desk."

Cutting a man's tongue out after killing him was usually the sign that the killers thought he was a snitch. An informant.

"Elmore—"

"The cops are comin'," Elmore said. "But I wanted to let you know."

"Because it's my fault?" Sangster asked. "If he hadn't helped me Primble wouldn't have had him killed."

"You think Primble did this?"

"Who else?"

"Well, it figures," Elmore said. "He and Primble haven't never seen eye to eye since Primble came to Vegas. And he did give that New Orleans cop Primble's name."

"Why did he do that?" Sangster asked. "It's probably what got him killed."

"Maybe."

Sangster was surprised the big black man wasn't blaming him.

"Don't take all the credit, my man," Elmore said. "B. Cool probably just took the opportunity to cause Primble some pain. After all, the Vegas cops don't bug him."

"They don't?"

"Not while they're on his payroll."

"Two detectives?"

"Ha!" Elmore said. "A lot more than that."

"Elmore, why would—"

"I gotta to go," Elmore said. "The cops are here."

"Call me later," Sangster said. "We'll meet up."

"You got it. We'll make the fuckers who did this pay."

Elmore broke the connection.

Make the fuckers pay. Wasn't that why Sangster had come to Vegas in the first place? Only he was trying to find a way to do it without killing. And he ended up getting B. Cool killed. That was the second person who died because he wasn't the man he used to be.

Was this what it meant to have a soul? He had to watch his friends die?

What had the Obeah Man told him? *"If your heart is true, and your soul is true, then whatever you perceive that you must do is true."*

He opened the gun box.

FORTY-TWO

Sangster sat in his room, waiting. It had grown dark outside, and he hadn't bothered to turn on a light. He just sat there, with the Webley Bulldog in his hand. It felt at once familiar, and alien. If he allowed himself to admit it, he might even say it felt good in his hand. But he couldn't do that.

He set it down.

His cell rang.

"Elmore?"

"Let's meet."

"You say where."

"There's a bar," Elmore said, "a dive, really."

"Tell me how to get there."

Sangster memorized the directions.

"I'll be getting rid of this phone," he told Elmore. "I've used it too long, so you won't be able to call me and cancel."

"I won't cancel," Elmore said. "I'll be there in one hour."

"See you there."

Sangster hung up, looked at the Bulldog on the coffee table, picked it up, put it back in the box, closed it, donned his UNLV cap and left the room, making sure his *Do Not Disturb* sign was out.

Calling the bar where he was to meet Elmore a dive was an understatement. On the bright side, the car he was driving fit right into the neighborhood.

He parked on the street several storefronts down from the bar, fairly certain no one would still be there when he came back. There was a pink neon sign just over the front door that said BAR.

As he entered, several patrons turned to take a have at him. Behind the bar was a flat screen TV with a fight going on. After making sure they didn't know him and deeming him unworthy of any more time, they turned back to watch the fight. He looked around and spotted Elmore sitting at a booth in the back. The black man saw him, but made no gesture. From the look on his face Sangster knew the man was not happy.

He walked to the booth and stopped.

"Have a seat," Elmore said. "Brew?"

"Sure."

Sangster sat down in the booth. Elmore waved and the bartender came over with a beer.

"I'm sorry about B. Cool," Sangster said, after the bartender withdrew.

"I don't want you to be sorry," Elmore said, "I want you to tell me what we're gonna do about it."

"We?"

"That's right," Elmore said. "You need somebody who knows the town. Even more now that Primble knows you're here."

"And how do you know that?"

"The word's gone out on you," Elmore said. "He's got eyes and ears everywhere lookin' for you."

"I figured."

"And that New Orleans cop," Elmore said. "I bet he's lookin' for you, too."

"You might be right."

"That name? Stark? That one of yours?"

Sangster didn't answer.

"Okay, never mind," Elmore said. "You need me, and I need my revenge."

"Why don't you just get another job," Sangster said, "or take over B. Cool's club?"

"Look," Elmore sad, "Cool was more than a boss to me."

"He was your friend?"

"I wouldn't go that far, but he gave me a chance when nobody else would," Elmore said. "He recognized me for what I was—a kid from the hood who made somethin' of himself. I got an education, and came back to establish myself. He was helpin' me, maybe groomin' me. I don't know if I'll be takin' his place or not. I can't worry about that now. But I know he has to be avenged."

"What makes you think I'm the man to do it?"

"He told me who you used to be," Elmore said. "He also said you had some kind of epiphany, that you're a new man. I don't care if you're an old man or new man, but I think you're the man to get this done."

"And you want to help."

"I do."

"And if it means killing somebody? Are you ready for that?"

"I am."

"I don't think you are, Elmore," Sangster said "Have you ever killed anyone before?"

Elmore answered honestly.

"No."

"Okay, then," Sangster said.

"But I can help."

"Yeah, you can."

"So you'll find Primble's men and kill them? I mean, that's what you came here to do, right?"

"I came here to do something," Sangster said, "to make a point."

"So make it."

Sangster didn't want to tell Elmore that he'd lost his way. He wasn't sure now what his point was or how to make it.

He sipped the beer, found it lukewarm.

"You shouldn't drink that," Elmore said. "It's like warm piss."

"Can you get me what I need, Elmore?"

"That depends," the big man said. "What do you need?"

"I need a safe house," Sangster said.

"I can do that."

"Away from the glitz and the lights."

"Away from Primble's eyes and ears."

"Exactly."

"And what else do you need?"

"Time," Sangster said.

He needed time to make a decision, and to come to terms with what he had to do.

"Done," Elmore said.

On the flat screen somebody got knocked out and a roar went up from the men at the bar.

FORTY-THREE

The next morning Sangster was waiting outside his hotel, in the back, with his suitcase on the ground at his feet, and the gun box that B. Cool had given him under his arm. There was no law against carrying the guns in a box. He decided to let Elmore pick him up rather than using Huntley again.

Elmore's Corvette pulled into the parking lot at 8:35 a.m. Sangster waved and Elmore pulled up alongside him. He got out and opened the trunk, picked up Sangster's suitcase and dropped it in. Meanwhile, Sangster got into the front seat, set the box in his lap.

"You ready?" Elmore asked, sliding in behind the wheel.

"I'm ready."

"Check out?"

"No," Sangster said. "They'll figure it out."

"What about the credit card you gave them?"

"They're going to be real disappointed when they try to run it."

"They didn't run it yet?"

"Just for the security deposit," Sangster said, "Fifty bucks. Any more than that and it's going to bounce sky high."

"You're not worried about that?"

"They'll be looking for a guy named Westlake. He doesn't exist anymore."

"Well, that's good."

"What's happening with the club?"

"It's open, running as usual, for now."

Sangster nodded.

"You want me to get you one of the girls?"

"No," Sangster said, "that's okay. I can get my own girls. Can we get going?"

"Sure," Elmore said. "Sure we can."

Elmore drove Sangster to a house in Henderson. It was on King Street, off the North Boulder Highway, a couple of blocks from a local place called The Mugshot Eatery and Casino.

As they drove past the Mugshot, Elmore said, "There's no table games there, just some slots and some real good food."

"I won't need any of it."

"A man's gotta eat."

"Well, if you stocked the place like I asked, I'll eat."

"Oh, it's stocked."

Elmore pulled in front of the house. It was a one-story A-frame that had been built in the 60's, renovated in the 80's and then again in the 2000's.

"It's been empty for a couple of years," Elmore said, turning off the motor. "I aired it out, though. Should smell okay."

"It'll be fine." Sangster held out his hand and Elmore dropped the keys into it.

"Come on, dude," Elmore said, "I'll carry your suitcase in."

It wasn't really a suitcase, more like an overnight bag. Sangster traveled light, bought what he needed when he needed it.

"I got it," he said. "There's no need for you to come in."

Elmore shrugged, opened the trunk, handed Sangster his bag.

"What about neighbors?"

"They won't bug you," Elmore said. "They're eighty years old."

"On both sides?"

"Give or take ten years."

"Okay." Sangster started up the walk to the door.

"When will I hear from you?" Elmore asked.

The ex-hitman turned and faced B. Cool's ex-right hand.

"When I've decided what to do."

"And when will that be?"

"Elmore," Sangster said, "just sit tight. I'll be in touch."

"Okay."

"And don't get killed."

Elmore was turning to walk to his car, but he stopped short and looked back.

"Why would I get killed?"

"I'm just saying don't," Sangster said. "I *am* going to need your help."

"Okay, Sangster," Elmore said. "I'll wait for your call."

Sangster nodded and went inside.

The cupboards were filled just the way Sangster had asked Elmore to fill them. Cans of soup—a half dozen different kinds—and cans of tuna. On the counter was a fresh loaf of bread and a can of coffee. There was a coffee maker there, as well. In the freezer were some frozen dinners—a half a dozen different kinds. There was also butter and milk. On top of the refrigerator were cereal boxes—three different kinds.

There was enough food there to last for as long as it would take Sangster to decide what he was going to do. For him to decide what he could live with and not lose his soul, again. He had spent too many years living without a soul and did not want to revert to that existence. But the fact remained, he now had to bring back a part of the man he used to be. Because the person he was now was too indecisive—and he didn't want to be that man, either.

Sangster needed to be reborn.

Yet again.

Sangster was able to come to terms with one thing. He'd been impatient, had pressed the matter and, in the end, had tipped off Primble that he was in town. So now he had to practice patience, lay low and get himself into shape—mentally and physically—to do what had to be done.

And patient he was.

But how patient would Primble and Telemaco be?

FORTY-FOUR

"It's been two weeks!" Primble shouted at Edgar, O'Malley and Guiliano. "Where the hell is he?"

The three men exchanged anxious glances, and then Guiliano said, "We don't know, boss."

"That's what I've been hearing," Primble said. "I'm not happy with that answer."

"What else can we do, boss?" O'Malley said. "If Sangster's in town, he's gone to ground."

"How?" Primble asked. "He doesn't know the town, and he doesn't have B. Cool to help him anymore."

Both O'Malley and Guiliano smirked at that. They'd been after their boss for a long time to let them take B. Cool out.

"What about Elmore?" Edgar asked.

"What about him?" Primble asked. "He's an idiot."

"He was B. Cool's right hand, and he has a degree in—" Edgar went on, but Primble cut him off.

"I said he's an idiot," Primble said. "All Jamaicans are."

"Boss," O'Malley said, "Elmore ain't from Jamaica."

"He might as well be," Primble said, dismissively. "What about the cop?"

"Which cop?" O'Malley asked.

But Edgar quickly said, "Detective Telemaco is still in Vegas."

"And what's he doing?"

The three men exchanged a glance again, and then Guiliano offered, "Waiting?"

"Why don't his bosses call him home?" Primble said.

"We don't know that—" O'Malley started.

"It was a rhetorical question!" Primble snarled.

O'Malley frowned, but before he could ask what that meant, Guiliano said to him, "Later."

"Okay," Primble said, "however many men we have looking for him, I want it doubled."

"That's gonna cost, boss," Guiliano said, knowing how frugal Primble was.

"No, it won't," Primble said to the three of them, "because if it takes much longer I'm going to start taking it out of your salaries! Now get out!"

Edgar ushered the two assassins from Primble's office, and when he turned to look at his master, Primble said, "You, too."

"Yessir."

Primble remained at his desk after his men left, brooding. Sangster was still in town. He knew it. By going to ground, he was trying to get under Primble's skin. What they needed to do was find out who had helped him. Who knew the town well enough to hide him from Primble's eyes and ears.

And then there was the cop.

Primble's normal way to handle cops who were annoying was to throw money at them. Perhaps that was what he had to do. Arrange a meeting with the New Orleans detective and see what his price was? And if he didn't have a price, then he wouldn't leave Primble much of a choice. But he'd make that decision when the time came.

In the entry foyer of the house, O'Malley and Guiliano stopped and waited for Edgar to catch up.

"You know, I ain't never asked," O'Malley said. "What's he got against Jamaicans?"

"Don't ask," Edgar said. "Don't ever ask."

"Well," Guiliano said, "he's wrong about Elmore. Just because he's black don't make him Jamaican, and he ain't dumb."

"No, he's not," Edgar said. "I would suggest you check on him, see if he's been seen with Sangster, maybe even follow him. He might lead you to Sangster."

"And then we can take him out," O'Malley said.

"And then you should call here and wait for instructions."

"From you?" O'Malley asked.

"From our employer," Edgar said.

"Yeah, okay, Edgar," Guiliano said, before O'Malley could say anything else dumb. "We'll do that."

Edgar opened the door and closed it firmly behind them.

"I don't like that guy," O'Malley said.

"Well, he had a good idea," Guiliano said. "We better take a good hard look at Elmore."

"He's keepin' the club open," O'Malley said. "You know, maybe we shoulda took him out when we took care of B. Cool."

"We don't take anybody out without instructions, Jimmy," Guiliano said. "The boss is really clear about that."

"Yeah, yeah," O'Malley said, "but Sangster...that should be a different story."

"Yeah," Guiliano said, "he probably should be."

FORTY-FIVE

The first week dragged by.

It was hard to make time pass when he was confined to one space.

The house was furnished. Sangster had comfortable places to sleep and sit. He had food, drink and books that he had asked Elmore for. He had a TV so he could watch local news. The rest of the time he did isometric exercises to get his body in shape. He didn't need any equipment for that, just walls, floors and his own resistance.

He spent some time looking out windows. The front gave him a view of the street, the neighborhood, the neighbors. There wasn't much activity—a few cars would go by, every so often somebody would pass on foot. The only people he saw regularly were the people who lived on either side. Elmore was right, they were elderly. On one side, a man who looked to be in his seventies, who went for a lot of walks. On the other side, a couple in their eighties, who never seemed to grow tired of sweeping their property.

The back window looked out over a yard that had fallen into great disrepair. It was just...brown.

He exercised and read most of the days. In the evenings he watched the news, then read some more or sat in the dark and considered his life and the direction it was taking.

He had one phone call that first week, from Elmore. It had come a few hours ago.

"Everything okay?" he asked.

"Fine."

"Need anything?"

"No."

"Well, everything's been quiet around here," the man said. "No sign of Primble or his people."

"Don't get complacent," Sangster told him.

"Oh, don't worry, I won't," Elmore said. "You make up your mind yet?"

"Not yet," Sangster said. "You'll know when I do."

"Well, that cop, Telemaco, is still around. He must have got himself a leave of absence or something."

"What's he been doing?"

"Nothin'," Elmore said. "Still stayin' in the same dump, only goes out to eat."

"He must be doing something," Sangster said. "He's got to have a smart phone or computer in that room with him."

"Maybe."

"Okay," Sangster said, "call me in another week—unless I call you first."

"Right."

He'd been sitting in the dark since then, thinking. He didn't know if he could make up his mind based on what the Obeah Man had told him. Maybe he needed to talk to somebody else. Somebody more traditional. A Catholic priest? A rabbi?

He was startled from his contemplation by the sound of raised voices that seemed to be coming from outside, in front of the house. He went to the front window and looked out. A man and a woman—or maybe a boy and a girl—were apparently engaged in an argument. But as he watched, the complexion of the encounter changed. The man grabbed the woman's arm obviously hurting her.

He didn't want to get involved in somebody else's problems—he had enough of his own, for the moment—

but he would not be able to concentrate as long as this was going on.

He went to the front door, opened it and stuck his head out.

"Hey," he called out, "take it somewhere else."

"Fuck you!" the man called back.

"Ow! Damn it, Zack, you're hurting me. Let go!"

Zack did as she asked, then backhanded her to the ground.

Sangster stepped outside and approached the two. The man was larger than him, ten years younger, but he was obviously a bully.

"That's enough," he said, "step away from the girl."

"I say when it's enough, friend," the man said. "Come closer and you'll get the same."

"I'm not a little girl, *friend*," Sangster said. "You'll find that I won't go down that easy."

"Zack—" the girl sobbed.

"Shut up!" Zack said, keeping his eyes on Sangster. "Come on, old man, let's see what you got."

Sangster's frustrations boiled to the top. He stepped within arm's reach of the man, waiting for him to reach out. He swatted the arm away, then stepped inside the man's reach, grabbed his arm, turned, jammed his shoulder into the man's armpit, rotated the arm and snapped it at the elbow. Sangster never indulged in long fights. He chose to put an end to them as soon as possible.

Instead of screaming the man's eyes popped and he gurgled. Sangster released his arm. Zack grabbed it, cradled it and staggered back. Sangster gave him credit for not crying out.

"Damn you!" Zack said. "You didn't have to do that."

"It was the lesser of two choices I could think of," Sangster said. "You better get to the hospital and have that set."

"I've had broken bones before," the man said. "I'll be back."

"Not anytime soon," Sangster said, knowing that by the time Zack *was* ready to come back, he'd be gone.

Still cradling his arm Zack skulked off, got into a car and drove away.

Sangster turned and looked down at the girl.

"You all right?"

"Y-yes."

"Can you get home?"

"I was—I was goin' in there," she said, pointing to the house where the octogenarian couple lived. "My grandparents live there."

"Okay." He started away.

"Wait—" She held her hand out to him.

"What?"

"I know you."

"No, you don't."

"I do," she said. "Help me up."

Reluctantly he reached down, clasped hands with her and pulled her to her feet. In so doing, her face was illuminated by a street lamp. She was right. She knew him, and he knew her.

It was Laurie, the waitress from the diner.

FORTY-SIX

Sangster took Laurie into his house and got her seated at the kitchen table. She had a spit lip, a bleeding, scraped knee and didn't want to wake her grandparents and worry them.

"I don't have a first aid kit," he said. "I'll get a damp wash cloth."

"Thank you."

He went to the bathroom, came back with the cloth and handed it to her. He was not the type—now or ever—to play nurse.

As she dabbed at her lips and knee, he said, "Something to drink?"

"Whataya got?"

"Water and coffee."

"That's it? No booze?"

"No booze."

"Coffee's good."

He went to the coffee maker on the counter and poured her a cup.

"Identity switch, huh?" she said with a smile, accepting the cup.

"I suppose."

She sipped the coffee, made a face and set the cup down.

"Where did you learn to do that?" she asked.

"Do what?"

"What you did to Zack."

"I learned a long time ago that in a fight, it's best to just get it done as soon as possible. Especially against a bigger opponent. Is he your boyfriend?"

"No," she said, "I broke a cardinal rule and ended up paying for it."

"What rule?"

"Not to date customers."

"Ah."

"Of course," she said, "with you and me, this isn't a date."

"No, it's not."

"We're neighbors, kind of," she said. "Speaking of which, how long have you lived here? I thought this house was empty."

"It was," he said. "I'm just renting it, been here about a week."

"Why?"

"Why what?"

"Why would you rent a house in this neighborhood?"

He shrugged and said, "It's quiet."

"What are you doin' that you need quiet?"

"Thinking."

"About what?"

"Life."

"Ah...I do that all the time. But never when it's quiet. Maybe that's why I haven't come up with any answers."

"I haven't either."

She folded the wash cloth so that the bloody side didn't show and set it down on the table.

"Thanks for that."

"I don't think you'll have to worry about Zack again for a while."

"No," she said, "I don't think he'll ever bother me again. But you, on the other hand..."

"By the time he heals, I'll be gone."

"He may not wait until he heals," she said. "He has friends."

"Shame on them."

"That's funny," she said. "You're funny, but I can tell you're not trying to be."

She cocked her head and studied him.

"What?"

"Just tryin' to figure you out."

"Don't," he said. "It won't be worth your time."

"Sorry," she said, "but you're not like anybody else. It sorta piques my interest."

"You better get some rest," he told her.

"Right," she said. "I have to get to work tomorrow."

He walked her to the front door.

"So how long will you be stayin' here?" she asked.

"Not long."

"Another...what? Few days? Week?"

"I'm not sure."

"Maybe we could...do somethin'?"

"What about your rule?"

"Ah, you know what they say about rules."

"Yes, well, I'm afraid I'm going to be busy."

"Right," she said, "all that thinkin'."

He didn't know what to say to that.

Three days later Edgar entered Primble's office. His boss looked up at him through bloodshot eyes.

"What?"

Edgar had never seen his boss looking like this. Sangster was really getting to him.

"We have put eyes and ears everywhere," Edgar said.

"And?"

"Three days ago a man walked into a hospital," Edgar said. "He was cradling a broken arm. One of our people talked to him, and when he described how his arm had been broken by a man smaller and older than he was, it sounded like a pro."

"What do I care about some arm breaker?"

"Sir, it happened in front of a house in a quiet neighborhood in Henderson. It's the perfect place for someone like Sangster to hide, in among what is mostly a senior population. And the man snapped the kid's arm with ease."

"We need more than that."

"The description," Edgar said. "The kid had a very good memory."

"And? Did he make a police report?"

"No," Edgar said, "he has a record and is intending to take his own revenge."

Primble got more excited the more he gave it thought. But why would Sangster, in hiding, come out and do such a thing?

"If this was Sangster," Primble said, "he may have just signed his own death warrant."

"Yes, sir."

"How badly does this kid want to get him?"

"Real bad."

"Bring him in, then," Primble said. "Bring him here to me."

"Yes, sir."

But Edgar didn't leave.

"Is there something else?"

"Yes, sir."

"Well, spit it out."

Edgar hesitated, then said, "We feel—Guiliano, O'Malley and I—that the man who helped Sangster go to ground was Elmore."

"I thought we settled that."

"Well, sir," Edgar said, carefully, "we knew you'd want to leave no stone unturned, so Guiliano and

O'Malley looked very carefully into all of Elmore's movements, of late."

"And?"

"It looks like he's planning a move to take over B. Cool's operation," Edgar said. "He could have used Cool's network to find Sangster a place to dig in."

Primble rubbed his chin. His eyes felt gritty and hot. If there was a time to grasp at straws, maybe this was it. A kid with a broken arm and a Jamaican—

"And he's not Jamaican?"

"Um, no, sir," Edgar said, "he's not."

"Okay, then," Primble said, "let's bring him in, too. Let's have a little talk with Mr. Elmore—is that his first name or last name?"

"First," Edgar said. "His last name's Washington."

Primble snorted. "That figures."

"Yes, sir. Sir, where do you want them brought?"

"Here," Primble said. "I want them right here, both of them."

"Yes, sir."

Primble stood.

"I'm going to take a shower. Let me know when they arrive."

"Of course, sir."

Edgar left his boss, a slight smile on his face. He'd played that just right.

FORTY-SEVEN

The cell rang late on the eleventh night he was in the house.

"Hello?"

"S-Sang—Sangster..."

The voice was faint, but recognizable.

"Elmore."

"Fucked up, man," Elmore said. "I—I—they fucked me up."

"Where are you?"

"The street..."

"Tell me where you are, Elmore," Sangster said, "I'll come and get you."

Elmore gave him directions with what sounded like his last breath, and Sangster ran from the house to his car...

He found Elmore in the doorway of what looked like an abandoned store. He pulled the car to the curb so that his headlights illuminated the doorway. At the last minute, he'd donned a windbreaker and stuck the Bulldog in the pocket. It weighed heavily there.

"Elmore!"

He rushed to the black man, who was lying in a fetal position. His face was bloody and battered and there were obviously a lot more injuries that Sangster couldn't see.

"Fucked me up, man," he said, blood bubbles popping between his lips.

"Who?"

"P-Primble's boys."

"I can't see—are you—what? Shot?"

"They cut me up pretty bad, man."

Sangster saw a cell phone on the ground next to Elmore. It had blood on it, obviously the one he'd used to call.

"Why didn't you call for an ambulance?" Sangster asked, reaching for the phone.

"N-no, no," Elmore said, swatting his hand away. "N-no good. I'm toast. I—I wanted to warn ya. T-they came for me, but they w-wanted to know where I s-stashed you." He grabbed Sangster's arm, held it tight. "I didn't tell 'em, man. I didn't tell 'em nothin'." He wasn't speaking like an educated man at this point. His speech had reverted to the street speak of his youth.

"I know you didn't," Sangster said. "I know it."

"B-bastards wanted to take me with them, I-I think they were gonna plant me in the desert, b-but I—I booked it, t-took off." He laughed, then grimaced as blood dripped from his mouth. He tightened his hold on Sangster. "Y-ya gotta get 'em, man. Ya g-gotta get 'em...for me and for B. Cool. Swear it!"

"I promise, Elmore," Sangster said, "I promise. Come on, man, let's get you to a hospital—" He started to try and get the big man to his feet, but Elmore suddenly went limp. His hand fell away from Sangster's arm.

He was right.

He was done.

He called Huntley.

He didn't have anybody else to call.

"I've got a problem," he said into his cell.

"You call de right mon," Huntley said. "Where you be?"

He started to give the cab driver directions, but Huntley cut him off and said, "Me know dat block, mon. I be right there."

"Bring plastic."

"What?"

"A roll of plastic," Sangster said and broke the connection. "Enough to wrap a body."

"Whatchoo say? Wrap wha—" But Sangster broke the connection.

The cab pulled up about half-an-hour later. Several cars had passed at that late hour, but Sangster had cut his headlights to leave Elmore's body in darkness. Now the cab's lights were illuminating it again.

Sangster hurried to Huntley can and said, "Cut your engine."

Huntley did, and they were in darkness again.

"Did you bring the plastic?"

"It's in the back," Huntley said. "Mon, whatchoo need plastic for?"

"Spread it over the back seat and I'll show you."

Huntley opened the back door on his side, unfurled the thick plastic roll. Sangster opened his side and helped the cab driver cover the seat as completely as they could.

"Mon," Huntley said, across the seat, "Me gettin' a bod feelin' 'bout dis."

"It's going to get worse," Sangster said, "Come with me."

He walked back to the doorway with Huntley following reluctantly. When the driver saw the body he stopped and staggered back a step or two.

"What the—mon, who is dat?"

"Someone I knew," Sangster said.

"Dat mon is dead, mon."

"He sure is."

Huntley pointed at Sangster and said, "Mon, me knew you wasn't no writer."

"First of all," Sangster said, "I didn't kill him. He called me for help. By the time I got here, it was too late."

"So what we do now?"

"We move him."

"You ain't gonna call the police, mon?"

"For reasons I can't go into now, Huntley, I can't do that."

"Then why not leave him here?" Huntley asked. "Somebody will find him."

"No," Sangster said, "nobody can find him."

"Why not?"

"Huntley," Sangster said, "I'm going to pay you to help me move him."

"Pay me?"

"Yes."

"How much, mon?"

"A lot."

"And where we takin' him?"

"That's what you're going to decide," Sangster said. "I need a place to put him where nobody will ever find him."

"Mon, me don't know..."

"Five thousand," Sangster said. "And when I have time, I'll explain it all to you."

Huntley looked nervous.

"Look," Sangster said, "I've got no one else to ask in this town. I need your help. Do you want more money?"

"Yeah, mon," the Jamaican said, "me always want more money...but me take the five grand."

"Good," Sangster said, "thank you, Huntley. Now, where do we take him?"

"Where else, mon?" Huntley said, waving his arm. "The desert."

FORTY-EIGHT

"We gonna need shovels, mon," Huntley said.

They had both carried Elmore's body to the car and set it on the back seat. Then they wrapped the plastic around him.

"We can't bring anyone else in on this," Sangster said. "Do you have shovels at home?"

"My cousin got one."

"Who's your cousin? Darrell?"

"Mahbee."

"The Obeah Man?"

"Yes."

"You didn't tell me he was your cousin."

"Me gots lots of cousins, mon."

"All right," Sangster said. "Let's go get the shovels. Just don't tell him what they're for."

"Right."

They got into the cab, Sangster counting them lucky that they hadn't been seen moving the body.

Huntley drove them to the Obeah Man's house, and Sangster waited in the car. He knew the cab driver could have been in the house calling the police, but he decided to trust him. After ten minutes he came trotting back to the car with two shovels, opened the trunk, dropped them in and got back behind the wheel.

"You ever been to the desert?" he asked Sangster.

"Not this one."

"Be real quiet. The desert. She too quiet."

"Does it scare you?"

Huntley didn't answer. He started the car, then drove.

"You want the radio on?" Huntley asked.

"No."

They'd been driving in silence until they reached the desert.

"Is the quiet getting to you?"

"Yeah, mon," Huntley said, "it gets to me. How about you talk to me?"

"About what?"

"You said you would tell me about it. Don't play dumb with me, mon."

"Yeah, yeah, all right," Sangster said. He took a moment to decide how much to tell him. "Look, I came to town looking for some men. Elmore—that's him in the back—he was helping me."

"And it got him killed?"

"Looks like."

"Me not wantin' ta get killed, mon."

"You won't."

"Yeah, but me helpin' you, too."

"The difference is, nobody knows you're helping me," Sangster said. "We'll just keep it that way."

"So why you want to see the Obeah Man?"

"I wanted to see a holy man," Sangster said. "You took me to your cousin."

"All right, so why you wantin' ta see a holy man?"

"I need to get some things clear in my head."

"About what?"

"Religion."

"What about it?"

"I don't know...everything. I don't know much about it. Never been a religious man. You?"

"Me got me beliefs," Huntley said.

"Yeah, well, I don't."

"Mahbee, he help you?"

"He answered some questions," Sangster said, "and he gave me some advice. Whether or not he helped me remains to be seen."

"You want to say somethin'?" Huntley asked.

"Like what?"

The black man shrugged. "Don't you usually say somethin' when you bury a friend?"

"He wasn't my friend," Sangster said. "He was just helping me."

Huntley looked down at the plastic wrapped man in the hole they had just dug.

"Well, you got to say somethin'."

"I told you," Sangster said, "I've never been religious. I don't know what to say."

They stood there, staring into the hole, neither of them speaking.

Suddenly, Sangster said, "I'm sorry, Elmore. Sorry you got killed. Sorry B. Cool is dead. Sorry Lily's dead. I'm just...sorry."

He picked up his shovel, tossed the first pile of dirt into the hole. He didn't like the sound it made when it hit the plastic.

"Come on," he said, "let's get this done. When we get back to town, I'll pay you."

"Me don't think I help you no more after dis, mon," Huntley said, shoveling dirt into the hole.

Sangster looked at the man beside him, "I don't blame you."

FORTY-NINE

Huntley drove Sangster back to his car in silence. He seemed to be brooding but when he did speak his Jamaican *patois* seemed to grow thicker with each word.

He pulled up in front of the building, behind Sangster's car. Huntley put the car in Park, but did not turn off the engine.

Sangster dug into his pockets to see how much money he had.

"I've got five hundred on me," he said, handing the money to Huntley. "We'll have to meet up so I can settle with you."

"Don't like dat," Huntley said, "but me got no choice."

"I'll call you," Sangster said. He got out of the car, slammed the door and leaned on it. "Thanks for all your help, Huntley."

"You don't get killed before you pay me, you hear?"

"I hear."

Still scowling, Huntley drove away.

Sangster got into his car and sat there for a few moments. His hands were sticky with Elmore's blood. He took something from the jacket of his windbreaker and saw that he still had Elmore's blood stained cell phone. He should have buried it with the man. He stuck it back in his pocket, determined to discard it where it would never be found at his earliest convenience.

He started the car, drove back to the house, parked in front but hesitated before getting out. He studied the house and the houses on either side. There was no movement in either of them. Finally he got out of the car, his hand around the Bulldog in his pocket.

At the front door, he used the key to open the door with his left hand, keeping his right hand on the gun. As he entered the house, he gripped the Bulldog tightly, but no one jumped out from behind the furniture. He turned on the lights, closed the door and relaxed a bit.

Then he took the Bulldog from his pocket and set it down on the table, next to the box that still held the Webley-Fosbery. The windbreaker was next, and he draped it over the back of a chair. He went to the refrigerator, got out a bottle of water and drank half of it down. Then he went to the kitchen sink and washed Elmore's blood from his hands.

But he couldn't. Oh, it came off, turned the water that was swirling in the sink red, but as he watched it go down the drain he knew he'd never be able to truly wash it off. He had Elmore's blood, Lily's blood and B. Cool's blood on his hands, and it was Primble's fault. Primble and his inept button men.

He dried his hands, picked up the bottle of water and finished it. He felt a coldness in the pit of his stomach that had nothing to do with the water he'd just drunk. It was a familiar coldness, though, the kind he hadn't felt for years. It was what he used to feel in his stomach when he was ready to get a job done...ready to kill.

He sat at the table and cleaned the guns, made sure they were in proper working order. It had been many years since he'd gone through this exercise, but it came natural to him. The guns felt good in his hands, the smell of the gun oil was like perfume in his nose.

He knew what he had to do. He just didn't know what it would do to his soul. The Obeah Man had said to do what was true.

* * *

Sangster wasn't sure what was true, but he knew what was right, and that was not letting Primble and his hitters kill any more innocent people.

The guns were clean and ready.

So was he.

He was not startled at all when someone started banging on the back door. Calmly, he picked up the Bulldog and went to see who it was. He stood to one side, pushed aside the curtain and peered out. It was the girl, Laurie. He thought about not answering, but she'd spotted him and began banging again.

He opened the door.

"Oh God!" she said, stumbling in.

"What is it?" He held the gun behind his back as he closed the door.

"I came to warn you," she gasped. "I thought maybe I was too late."

"Too late for what?" Sangster asked. "Warn me about what?"

"Can I have some water?"

"Sure."

She sat down at the table to catch her breath, accepted a bottle of water from him. He twisted the cap off for her, not to be polite, but to save time.

"I hurried here from work," she said, after a large gulp.

"Why?'

"I got a call from Zack. Remember Zack?"

"I remember."

"Well, he says you're gonna pay for what you did to him. He called you my 'new boyfriend' and said I better not be around, because the people who are comin' for you are gonna kill you."

"What people?"

"I don't know," she said.

"Well, what else did he say?" Sangster asked, "Exactly."

"Somethin' like 'they been lookin' for him and he's gonna get what's comin' to him."

There were only two people in town who were looking for him, and only one of them wanted to kill him.

Primble.

FIFTY

"You're what?" Laurie asked. "I don't think I heard you right."

"I'm going to wait right here."

"Somebody's comin' to kill you, and you're gonna wait for them?"

"That's right."

"That's crazy."

"What would be crazy is if you were still here when they arrive," Sangster said. "I want you to go next door, get your grandparents and take them somewhere."

"This late? They're probably in bed."

"Wake them up and get them out."

"Where should I take them?"

"You got any other family in town?"

"No, they're it," she said. "That's why I come and see them a lot."

"Well, if you want to keep on seeing them, take them somewhere...anywhere."

"I guess I could take them to my place."

"That's good," he said. "Take them there." Just somewhere out of the line of fire, he thought. "What about the people on the other side?" he asked her.

"Oh, that's Mr. Keats. He's out with his son."

"How do you know that?"

"It's Wednesday night," she said. "His son always takes him out on Wednesday night."

"Okay, then it's time for you to go." He took her by the arm with his left hand. As he did, his right hand came around from behind his back and she saw the gun.

"Who are you?" she asked. "I mean really."

"Nobody you'd ever want to know," he told her. "Not under normal circumstances."

She studied him for a moment, then nodded her head, as if she had come to a decision.

"Well," she said, "I guess these aren't normal circumstances, are they? Whoever's lookin' for you, Zack gave you up because of me. So I'm glad I warned you."

"So am I," he said. "Now go. Get your grandparents to a safe place."

"Okay," she said. He opened the door for her. Before going out she said, "You be careful."

"That's not what this is about."

After she left he went through the house and turned all the lights on. That would let them know he was home, but not what room he was in.

He picked out a corner of the living room, crouched there with a Webley in each hand and waited...

Primble looked at the men who were gathered in his living room. O'Malley, Guiliano and four more gunmen in his employ. Edgar was standing apart from them.

"Any sign of him?" he asked.

"No, sir," Guiliano said. "Nobody has seen him."

"He's dead," O'Malley said.

"What did you say?" Primble asked.

"He's dead," O'Malley said again, "he's gotta be."

"Did you see the body?"

"Well, no—"

"Then shut the fuck up!"

One of the other gunmen giggled.

"Is this funny to you?" Primble shouted. "There's a man out there whose intention is to kill me. That's funny to you?"

"No, sir."

"Then shut your fucking mouth, too."

The man looked down and didn't speak again.

"All right," Primble said, "you're going to this house in Henderson and see if the man living there is Sangster. And if he's there, you're going to kill him, and bring his body back to me. Understood?"

"Yes, sir," Guiliano said.

"I'm not going to accept any excuses," Primble said. "He'd better not jump out of a fucking moving car. Understood?"

"Yessir," O'Malley said

"Boss," Guiliano said, "what makes you think this guy is him?"

"The move he used on the kid," Primble said, "to break his arm? I've seen him do that before." He looked at O'Malley. "He likes to use limbs to finish fights fast. You should appreciate that."

O'Malley's knee ached at the mention of it.

"Yes, sir."

"Now understand this," Primble said. "This man is the finest killing machine I have ever seen. It comes natural to him. He may have been out of the game for a few years, but don't make any mistakes 'cause if you do, you'll be dead."

"Understood," Guiliano said.

"Silk, you and O'Malley are responsible for this," Primble said. "If you don't come back here with Sangster's body, don't come back at all. Understand?"

"Yessir."

"Now get out. Get it done."

"Let's go, boys," Guiliano said to the others.

They filed out of the room, and Edgar walked them to the door.

Primble had a drink in his hand when Edgar returned.

"Once they kill Sangster," he asked, "what do we do about the cop?"

"Nothing," Primble said. "He'll never find Sangster."

"What about Guiliano and O'Malley."

Primble gave Edgar a meaningful look and said, "He'll never find them either."

Edgar hesitated a moment, then said, "Understood."

Edgar turned to leave, but stopped, turned back.

"Sir?"

"Yes?"

"You know Sangster's real name, don't you?"

"Oh, yes," Primble said, "I know his real name."

"Then, why do you refer to him as Sangster?"

"That's the name he's chosen," Primble said. "A man's got a right to live by whatever name he chooses...or die by it."

FIFTY-ONE

Sangster rediscovered his patience that night, but did he lose his soul? That remained to be seen.

He put aside all the questions for later. On this night there was only...well, this night. He did, however, turn his eyes to the sky and ask...who? God? Someone...for a sign that this was the right thing to do.

He knew when they came they'd enter by then front and the back at the same time. He thought about turning off the lights, letting his eyes get used to the dark, but that would only make them more careful. He wanted them feeling confident—arrogant, even.

They'd die easier, that way.

They parked their cars down the block, approached the house on foot.

"It's all lit up," O'Malley said.

"That's good," Guiliano said. "If it was dark his eyes would be used to it, and ours wouldn't."

"You think he's really in there?" one of the other men asked.

"Well," O'Malley said, "his lights are on, and there's a car in front."

"Houses on each side look quiet," another man said.

"That's good," O'Malley said.

"Jimmy," Guiliano said, "take Ted and Bill and go around back."

"Okay, Silk."

"Start counting," Guiliano said. "We go in at one hundred."

"Counting when?" Ted asked.

"Now," Guiliano said.

O'Malley and the two men faded into the darkness, heading for the back.

"What are we supposed to do when we get inside, Silk?" Al Dexter asked.

"We're supposed to kill 'im, you simple sonofabitch," Guiliano said. "Now shut up. I'm counting."

Sangster closed his eyes.

He heard them coming.

He took out his last disposable cell and dialed the number of Telemaco's motel.

"Yes?" Telemaco said, when the connection was made.

"It's me."

There was a moment's hesitation then the New Orleans cop said, "I've been waitin' for you."

"Take down this address," Sangster said. "You'll find something there you've been looking for."

"You?"

Sangster broke the connection.

"...ninety-eight, ninety-nine...a hundred," Guiliano said.

He kicked in the front door as O'Malley kicked in the back. The six men rushed into the house with their guns in their hands.

***

Sangster was in the living room. The front and back doors may have flown open at the same time, but the men in the back were in the kitchen, where they could do no harm for a short time.

The first three—led by Guiliano—entered the living room, where Sangster needed only to raise the two Webleys.

The Bulldog was made for close up service, while the Fosbery was crafted for accuracy. It was also used mostly for target shooting, as it needed to be cocked each time before it was fired. Sangster had it cocked and ready, fired the first of the eight loads.

The Bulldog was a five shot weapon and could be fired simply by pulling the trigger. He would empty this weapon before cocking and firing the Fosbery again.

It took Guiliano and the other man a few seconds to locate Sangster. They turned to aim their weapons at him...and the lights went out.

Sangster didn't expect it, but he froze.

They were pointing their guns at him. He rose from his crouch with a gun in each hand and froze. He couldn't do it.

Until the lights went out.

He took it as a sign.

The black-out caused Guiliano and his men to hesitate. They were backlit by the moonlight coming in the open door, but the sudden darkness left them blind.

Sangster's first shot hit Guiliano in the forehead, snapping his head back. The second man was hit in the chest. The third man, realizing what was happening, said, "Aw, shit."

Sangster put a bullet in his chest.

***

O'Malley led the way into the house, stopped short when he saw that they were in the kitchen. He looked around, but there was nobody in the room but him and his two men. Then the lights went out, and they heard the shots from elsewhere in the house.

"Silk?" he shouted. "Silk, did you get 'im?"

Sangster moved quickly. He stepped over the bodies and went out the front door. He tucked the Fosbery into his belt, replaced the spent loads in the Bulldog with live ones as he worked his way around to the rear of the house.

"Silk?" he heard someone call from inside the house.

He got to the back door and entered.

And the lights came back on...

O'Malley waved to his men and they moved across the kitchen to the doorway. They went through, across a small dining room—slamming into the furniture in the dark—then to the living room, where they saw the three bodies on the floor as the lights came back on.

"Oh damn..." O'Malley said.

He turned, but knew he was too late...

Sangster came through the door from the kitchen to the dining room, crossed quickly, drawing the already cocked Fosbery from his belt. He saw the look of shock on the faces of the three men as they turned and recognized O'Malley from New Orleans.

He fired with both hands, and the men died quickly and with a flash of fear and disappointment...

* * *

Sangster packed his bag and ran out to his car. He didn't know for sure how long it would take for Telemaco and other cops to arrive, and he still had things to do that night.

As he started the car and drove away he realized tears were streaming down his cheeks.

FIFTY-TWO

Telemaco entered the house behind Las Vegas Detectives Crichton and Dudgeon. They stepped around the bodies.

"Do you know who these guys are?" Telemaco asked.

"Some of them," Dudgeon said. "That's Silk Guiliano."

"One of the men I've been looking for," Telemaco said. "What about O'Malley? Is he here?"

"Over here," Crichton said.

"Dead?" Dudgeon asked.

"As a mackerel."

Dudgeon turned another body over. "Bill Timlin."

"What about the others?" Telemaco asked.

"Don't know, but they must all work for Primble," Crichton said.

"Who did this?" Dudgeon asked, "Your man Stark?"

"Well," Telemaco said, "he did call me and tell me I'd find something I'm looking for here."

Crichton said, "Guess he was right. We better search the house. Maybe he's in another room, dead."

The three detectives did a quick search, came up with nothing. They met back in the living room, among the bodies.

"No sign of him," Crichton said. "No clothes, not even a sock."

"He did this," Telemaco said, "and then left."

"To go where?" Dudgeon said.

"I might have an idea."

"I've got to call this in," Crichton said, taking out his cell phone, "and then we'll listen to your idea."

"It might not be so smart to wait—" Telemaco said.

Crichton raised a finger to Telemaco and spoke into his phone...

Sangster drove to Green Valley, stopped the car down the street from Primble's front gate. He took both guns out and made sure they had full loads. On the way over, he tried to figure out the best place to go over the wall. While he was inside before, he never saw a likely place. Maybe there was a spot on the outside. Now he realized he didn't have much time. Once the cops saw the mess he left at the house in Henderson, it was only a small jump to realize he'd come here.

He started the car again. The best way in was through the front door.

Primble entered the security room.

"What's so important?" he demanded of Edgar, who was seated in front of the monitors.

"The new sensors have detected a vehicle by the west wall."

"What's it doing?"

"It's just...parked."

"Let me see the front gate."

Edgar hit a button and the front gate came into view just as a car drove right through it.

"What the fuck—" Primble said, leaning over and peering at the screen.

Sangster floored the gas pedal when he had the car pointed at the gates. He didn't know what would happen when the rattle trap struck the iron bars, so he braced himself. The front end of the car struck at high speed, and they snapped open. The car shuddered, but kept on going. He let out a whoop as he drove up the drive to the house.

He was feeling invigorated, like he hadn't felt in some time.

"It's him!" Primble said. "Call Silk and O'Malley. Get them back here."

Edgar turned in his chair and looked at his boss.

"If he was ever as good as you say," Edgar said, "they're dead. And now he's coming for you."

"How long before security gets here?"

"They usually respond in minutes."

"Can you keep him away from me for that long?"

"Probably."

"I'll be in my office," Primble said, "with a gun. Let me know it's you before you come in so I don't blow your head off."

"Right."

Primble left the room. Edgar got up, walked to one of the walls, opened a door there. Inside was a small room filled with guns. He picked out an AK-47, checked it, then closed the door.

Sangster knew this had to be done before the security company responded to the alarm.

He stopped the car in front of the house, ran around to the side, where he knew there were a pair of French doors. Since the alarms were no longer a concern he picked up a metal patio chair and tossed it through the door glass. He went through before the glass even stopped cascading to the floor. He had the Fosbery cocked and in his hand, and the Bulldog in his belt.

He hadn't seen the inside of the house before, but that was okay. He didn't think he'd have to look for Primble. It was more likely somebody would come looking for him.

The room he was in was a dining room, with a large, marble table. He tested the table's weight to see if he could overturn it, but it weighed a ton.

"Hard to budge, isn't it?" a voice asked.

He turned quickly, saw an older man holding an AK-47. Oddly, the weapon was aimed at the ceiling. The man had the drop on him.

"You're wondering how I knew you'd come in this way," the man said. He shrugged. "It just made sense."

"How..." Sangster started.

"There's a hidden door behind that full length mirror. Don't feel bad. The only reason I got the drop on you is because you didn't know it was there. And maybe you're a little out of practice."

Sangster looked at the AK-47. He thought he could raise the Fosbery and fire before the man could level it at him. But even if he squeezed the trigger a millimeter as he died, the gun would spray the room with bullets.

"Take it easy, Sangster," the man said.

"What's your name?" Sangster asked.

"I'm Edgar," the man said. "Not my real name, though, no more than yours is Sangster. But, believe it or not, I used to be you. Yup, Primble's go to boy. But that was a long time ago. Now he keeps me around as a butler. Oh, he gives me some work to do in security, but to him I'm the butler."

"So, what?" Sangster asked. "Kill me and he'll let you back into the inner circle."

"No," Edgar said, "you kill him and we'll all breathe a lot easier. Silk and O'Malley?"

"Both dead," Sangster said. "Along with the men they brought with them."

Edgar smiled. "Primble underestimated you. Now, don't get nervous. I'm gonna fire this AK into the ceiling."

Edgar pulled the trigger and peppered the ceiling with holes. Plaster rained down on him.

"There," he said, tossing the AK-47 away. "Now he thinks I killed you."

"And what am I supposed to do?"

"I don't know," Edgar said, "but you better do it fast. You've got maybe two minutes before the security company responds. Come on, I'll show you where he is."

Edgar led the way out of the dining room, across the entry foyer, to a hallway.

"Door at the end."

Sangster knew the man could be sending him into a trap, but he didn't really think so.

"Why are you doing this?"

"I told you," Edgar said. "He made me his *butler*."

Sangster nodded, getting it.

"Go on," Edgar said. "He's expecting me."

Sangster nodded and started down the hall...

FIFTY-THREE

Not only did the security company respond, but the police drove up soon after. It was Telemaco who figured this would be Sangster's next stop.

Crichton and Dudgeon flashed their tin at the security men and were allowed inside. Telemaco followed.

"How many bodies?" Dudgeon asked.

"One," the man said, "down that hall."

The three detectives walked down the hall, found another security man at the door of a room the Las Vegas detectives recognized as Primble's office.

Primble was seated behind his desk, a neat bullet hole between his eyes, which seemed to be wide with surprise. The blood had rolled down his nose and dripped off. There was a gun in the top drawer of the desk, but he'd never gotten to it.

"This was your guy?" Crichton asked Telemaco.

"I don't know," Telemaco said. "Maybe a turf war?"

"Well," Dudgeon said, "B. Cool was killed a while ago and his man Elmore just last night, so...maybe." He looked at his partner.

"Yeah," Dudgeon said, "maybe."

The two detectives knew they'd be making less money for a while, until somebody picked up the slack.

"Well," Telemaco said, "I'll leave you to it."

"You done?" Dudgeon asked.

"My two guys were in that other house," Telemaco said. "This was their boss, right?"

"Yep," Crichton said.

"Then I'm done," Telemaco said. "I'll be heading home tomorrow."

"Hope you enjoyed your stay in Las Vegas," Dudgeon said.

"It was great," Telemaco said. "If you guys are ever in New Orleans, I'll try to show you the same hospitality."

As he left the house the two Vegas detectives weren't quite sure what he meant by that.

When Telemaco entered his motel room Sangster said, "Don't turn on the light."

"You got a gun?" Telemaco asked.

"Two," Sangster said. "You?"

"Not licensed to carry in this town."

"That doesn't mean you don't have one."

"Well, I don't."

"Have a seat."

Telemaco could make Sangster out in the dark now. He was sitting in the corner in a chair. He took the only other seat, the bed.

"What's on your mind?" Telemaco asked.

"That's what I wanted to ask you."

"Those men in that house," the New Orleans detective asked, "they the ones killed Lily Devereaux?"

Sangster wasn't sure, but he thought that was the first time he'd heard Lily's last name.

"Yes."

"And they worked for the man in the big house. Primble?"

"That's right."

"And he had them kill her because he had a beef with you."

"Right, again."

"Well," Telemaco said, "seems to me they all got what was coming to them."

"Does that mean you're not coming after me?"

"For what?" Telemaco said. "Could I prove anything?"

"I'm sitting here with two guns."

"Not my town," Telemaco said. "You can drive a tank down the strip for all I care."

Sangster was silent for a few moments, then asked, "Is this on the level?"

"Yes."

"Because I may want to go back to Algiers," Sangster said. "Any objection to that?"

"As long as you don't kill anybody there," Telemaco said, "no."

"Then I'm going to leave now."

"Be my guest."

Telemaco heard a sound, like metal on wood.

"Don't leave those guns here. Bury them somewhere in the desert."

Sangster picked them up. The detective was right. They could be linked to half a dozen killings—and Primble.

Jesus, he was out of practice.

After Sangster left the room, Telemaco turned the light on and packed. He'd use his open-ended ticket to take a flight home tomorrow.

EPILOGUE

As Sangster walked up the path to the front door of his house in Algiers, he saw retired Sheriff Burke sitting there with the chess set.

Coming out of Primble's house he realized his rattle trap of a car was done, but he'd parked it behind a Jaguar that must have belonged to Primble. He'd found the keys in the visor, which nobody did anymore. Another sign?

He'd driven from Las Vegas to New Orleans, burying the guns along the way, as Detective Telemaco had suggested. All he had with him now was one overnight bag. He'd left the Jag on the ferry with the keys in it.

"What the hell—" he said. "How'd you know I'd be back today?"

"I didn't," Burke said, staring at the board. "To tell you the truth, I spend most of my afternoons over here. I like this porch better than mine."

Sangster sat down across from Burke, setting the bag on the deck.

"Set 'em up," he said.

"You want white?" Burke asked.

"Sure."

Sangster came out of the shower, walked naked into the bedroom, carrying a towel. He'd missed this old house.

Clean-shaven now, dressed in jeans, T-shirt, flip-flops, he walked into the living room, sat on the sofa and rubbed his face vigorously. Though he didn't usually watch TV, he needed something to occupy his mind, so he picked up the remote. In the morning he'd hit a pharmacy, find something there to help stay awake.

He'd killed again, something he'd sworn he'd never do. On that day, three years ago, he had awakened to find he had a soul.

Now he was afraid to go to sleep, for fear that he would wake up once again without one.

ABOUT THE AUTHOR

Randisi is the author of the "Miles Jacoby," "Nick Delvecchio," "Gil & Claire Hunt," "Dennis McQueen," "Joe Keough," and "The Rat Pack," mystery series. THE HONKY TONK BIG HOSS BOOGIE, the first book in the Auggie Velez Nashville P.I. series, appeared in 2013. UPON MY SOUL is the first book in the "Hitman with a Soul" Trilogy. He is the editor of over 30 anthologies. All told he is the author of over 600 novels.

He is the founder of the Private Eye Writers of America, the creator of the Shamus Award, the co-founder of Mystery Scene Magazine.

MYSTERIES BY ROBERT J. RANDISI

The Miles Jacoby Series
Eye in the Ring
The Steinway Collection (aka Beaten to a Pulp)
Full Contact
Separate Cases
Hard Look
Stand Up

The Nick Delvecchio Series
No Exit from Brooklyn
The Dead of Brooklyn
The End of Brooklyn

The Gil & Claire Hunt Series
Murder is the Deal of the Day
The Masks of Auntie Laveau
Same Time, Same Murder

The Joe Keough Series
Alone with the Dead
In the Shadow of the Arch
Blood on the Arch
East of the Arch
Arch Angels
Back to the Arch (forthcoming)

The Dennis McQueen Series
The Turner Journals
Cold-Blooded

The Rat Pack Series
Everybody Kills Somebody Sometime
Luck be a Lady, Don't Die
Hey You, with the Gun in Your Hand
You're Nobody til Somebody Kills You
I'm a Fool to Kill You
Fly Me to the Morgue
It was a Very Bad Year
You Make Me Feel So Dead
The Way You Die Tonight

The Auggie Velez/Nashville Series
The Honky Tonk Big Hoss Boogie
The Last Sweet Song of Hammer Dylan
The Festival of Death (working title)

Stand Alone Crime Novels
The Disappearance of Penny
The Ham Reporter
Curtains of Blood
The Offer
The Bottom of Every Bottle
The Picasso Flop

Collections
Delvecchio's Brooklyn
The Guilt Edge

OTHER TITLES FROM DOWN AND OUT BOOKS

See www.DownAndOutBooks.com for complete list

By J.L. Abramo
Catching Water in a Net
Clutching at Straws
Counting to Infinity
Gravesend
Chasing Charlie Chan
Circling the Runway (*)

By Trey R. Barker
2,000 Miles to Open Road
Road Gig: A Novella
Exit Blood

By Richard Barre
The Innocents
Bearing Secrets
Christmas Stories
The Ghosts of Morning
Blackheart Highway
Burning Moon
Echo Bay
Lost (*)

By Milton T. Burton
Texas Noir

By Reed Farrel Coleman
The Brooklyn Rules

By Tom Crowley
Vipers Tail

By Jack Getze
Big Numbers
Big Money
Big Mojo (*)

By Keith Gilman
Bad Habits

By Jon & Ruth Jordan
Murder and Mayhem in
Muskego (Editors)

By Bill Moody
Czechmate
The Man in Red Square

By Gary Phillips
The Perpetrators
Scoundrels (Editor)

By Lono Waiwaiole
Wiley's Lament
Wiley's Shuffle
Wiley's Refrain
Dark Paradise

(*)—Coming Soon